Praise for *Mommy's Angel*

"Miasha keeps things moving at a fast clip, but the basic empathy and understanding that pervade are the story's real appeal. [She] never loses sight of the basic humanity of all the lost souls that surround Angel."   —*Publishers Weekly*

"In the midst of all the same voices in literature, Miasha brings authenticity to the pages of this novel. She's the crème de la crème—enjoy!"

—Vickie M. Stringer, *Essence* bestselling author of
Let That Be the Reason

"*Mommy's Angel* highlights some of the harsh realities that many of our society's poor and forgotten children face in life. . . . Earthy, realistic, and full of unpredictable twists and turns, Miasha has written a novel that is sure to please."

—R.A.W. Sistaz

"*Mommy's Angel* is a fast-paced, well-written, realistic view of what addiction does to our communities. It sheds a bright light on how the addict's hurt, pain, and trouble are recycled onto the people closest to them."

—Danielle Santiago, author of *Grindin'* and
Essence #1 bestseller *Little Ghetto Girl*

"A poignant tale of innocence lost in Brooklyn."
—K'wan, author of *Gangsta, Street Dreams, Eve,* and *Hood Rat*

"Miasha enters the arena of urban literature full throttle and ready to swing . . . surely to become one of the most-talked-about novels of 2006." —Mahogany Book Club, Albany, NY

"Miasha cooks up a delicious drama with all the ingredients of a bestseller—seduction, vindication, and lots of scandal."
—Brenda L. Thomas, author of *Threesome, Fourplay,* and *The Velvet Rope*

"Miasha tells it like it is. Her writing style is gritty and gripping, and will keep you reading and wanting more."
—Karen E. Quinones Miller, author of *Ida B*

"Miasha writes with the fatal stroke of a butcher knife. This book is raw material. Squeamish readers beware. You want proof? Just read the first page."
—Omar Tyree, *New York Times* bestseller and NAACP Image Award–winning author of the Flyy Girl trilogy

"With *Secret Society,* readers should be prepared to expect the unexpected. Each page is a roller coaster ride of emotion, drama, and intrigue. Miasha packs her debut novel with so many scandalous scenarios that the reader can't help but anxiously turn the page in anticipation. An excellent debut that still has me shaking my head in amazement, long after I read the last page!"
—Tracy Brown, bestselling author of *Dime Piece, Black,* and *Criminal Minded*

"Miasha writes with fire in this tale of two girls with a shocking secret and a story told with raw, heartfelt drama that is sure to carve this first-time novelist a place in the urban lit world."
—Crystal Lacey Winslow, bestselling author of *Life, Love & Loneliness*

ALSO BY MIASHA

Secret Society
Diary of a Mistress
Mommy's Angel

Sistah
FOR SALE

Miasha

A Touchstone Book
Published by Simon & Schuster
New York   London   Toronto   Sydney

 Touchstone
A Division of Simon & Schuster, Inc.
1230 Avenue of the Americas
New York, NY 10020

TOUCHSTONE and colophon are registered trademarks
of Simon & Schuster, Inc.

Designed by Jamie Kerner-Scott

Manufactured in the United States of America

ISBN-13: 978-0-7394-9399-1

I am dedicating this one to all my fans worldwide. If not for you, there would be no way I'd be able to put out so many books in such a short time. Enjoy this one and the next and all the ones to come!

CHAPTER 1

The day started off different from any other. First of all, we slept in a hotel the night before, which was rather strange seeing as though we had an apartment just blocks away. Then, that morning my mom woke me up and dressed me quickly while my dad loaded up his friend's car with our suitcases. My mom sat me on her lap in the backseat of my dad's friend's car. My dad sat in the passenger seat. It was so early in the morning that I could see the sun rising over the palm trees as we drove away from the hotel. I remember thinking about how beautiful the sight was and then falling asleep in my mother's arms.

When I was awakened by my mom we were at a small airport. My dad's friend had stopped the car and he and my dad got out and started taking our suitcases from the trunk. There was a small plane on the ground just a few feet from where we were parked. It was like a big open parking lot and all that was in it was the car we were in and the small plane my dad and his friend were transferring our bags onto. My mom carried me out of the car and over to the plane. There were two men already on board whom I never saw before, but my mom and dad apparently knew them well as they greeted each other with hugs. One man helped my mother and me onto the plane while the other went to the cockpit. My father hugged his friend as if he was saying farewell and then joined my mom and me. A big smile on his face, my dad caressed my mother's knee, then kissed her on the lips. I turned my head to look out the window as the plane started to slowly pull away. My dad reached down and tickled my stomach, bringing my attention back to him. I laughed so hard and tried to resist, prying his big hands off my tiny body every chance I could.

"Mommy, help me!" I squealed, squirming around on my mother's lap.

My mom just laughed along. Soon tears started rolling down my cheeks I was laughing so hard. Then my dad stopped, calling himself giving me a break. I wiped my eyes and was trying to catch my breath when the plane took off. The sudden increase in speed and the force of the plane lifting off the ground took me by surprise. I started choking on my own air. My mom immediately started to pat my back and my dad lifted my arms up over my head.

"Enough already. You're going to kill the poor child," the man who had helped us on the plane said.

I stopped choking and laid my head back against my mom's breasts. I remember looking at the man and wondering if he was serious about what he said about my dad killing me. I waited for him to smile or laugh and when he didn't I concluded that he was a bad man. I rolled my eyes at him and turned on my side so I wouldn't have to look at him. My mom adjusted me on her lap to suit my new position and before long I was asleep again.

Boom!

"Aaarrrr! Aaarrrr! Aaaarrrrr!"

I woke up to the echoing sound of a gunshot and the screeching sound of my mother's screams. I burst into tears at the sight of my father slumped over in his seat beside my mother and me. Blood was splattered all over my mom's clothes and I could feel it on my head and face. My mother tried to jump from her seat but was held down by the seat belt. Startled and panicked, she was unable to unbuckle it no matter how many times she tried.

"Shut up!" the bad man shouted to my mother, still holding the gun that he had used on my father.

"What you do that for? What wrong with you?!" my mother shouted in broken English.

"I said shut up!" the man shouted back, knocking my mother in the mouth with the butt of the gun.

I wanted to scream when I saw my mother's head fall back against the seat of the plane, but somehow I didn't. I guess I was afraid that I would suffer the same punishment if I did scream. So instead, I squeezed my eyes shut and cried as quietly as I could. I only opened them slightly when I heard my mom going off again.

"Nooo! Noooo! Please no! Please! Oh God noooo! Cliff! Cliff, help us!!" my mom yelled, a tooth falling from her bloody mouth.

I followed my mom's eyes and saw the man dragging my father toward an opened door on the plane. I turned my body around and jumped in my mother's arms with my knees in her lap. I squeezed her so tight and buried my tear-covered face in her chest. Muffling my voice, I screamed, "Daddy!" And that was it. I felt my mother's body jerk forward as she finally broke free of the seat belt. She dropped to the floor and practically crawled over to the door. With me still in her arms she tried to throw herself from the plane. It took the man hitting her again with the butt of the gun to keep her back, but that time he hit her in the head. She fell backward and I was on top of her. I was crying uncontrollably while maintaining my grip on her.

I was scared for my life. I didn't know if the man was going to throw me off the plane next or if he was going to hit me with the gun. All I knew was that he had killed my father and there was no telling what else he was capable of. I clung to my mother for dear life. I could feel her heart beating so I knew she was still alive, but I hoped and prayed that she stayed unconscious so that she wouldn't get hit again. As I lay there on top of my mother in the aisle of the small plane, I noticed that we were landing. The wheels hit the ground with such power and the plane started to decelerate. Once we came to a complete stop, I heard the man's footsteps walking in my mom's and my direction. My heart was pounding and the tears were gushing out. I had no idea what the man was going to do to us. I closed my eyes and held my mom tight, then I felt him pulling me.

At that point I didn't know what else to do but scream. He was taking me from my mother and most likely was going to kill her, too. I yelled out to my mother, screaming for her to wake up, begging her to help me. She didn't budge. I didn't give up though, because I knew she wasn't dead. I knew I felt her breathing under me. I just needed her to wake up. I knew if she had woken up she would have fought for me. She wouldn't have let the man take me away. But no matter how loud I screamed and how much I pleaded, my mother remained unconscious. I was taken off the plane and put inside an empty shack where I was gagged and bound to a chair. My tiny teeth sank into a dusty bandanna. My eyes were covered with a blindfold. My little wrists and ankles were held together by duct tape. I was left alone, scared and confused. I just knew my life was about to be over and that's a hell of a feeling for anyone to have, let alone a five-year-old.

I didn't know how many days went by, but I knew I was hungry and dehydrated. I felt like I had lost every bit of my energy, like I was dying. I felt myself drifting off to sleep when the door opened. I had to squint because even through the blindfold the beaming sunrays bothered my eyes, now so used to pitch darkness. I heard two sets of footsteps coming toward me and I tried to muster the strength to scream and move around, hoping to get whoever's attention. But then I heard the voice of the man who had killed my dad and I froze with fear.

"Her father was killed and her mother was deported back to the Dominican Republic. I figured with what you're doing, you could take her. She's young and fresh, perfect for your business. I'll give 'er to you for little money, too."

"Let's talk outside," an unfamiliar male voice suggested.

I was frightened beyond words. I didn't know what the men were plotting. Their footsteps headed away from me and it got dark again. I was trying to think of something to do or say to get their attention, particularly the attention of the unfamiliar male. At that point I would have gone with anyone if it meant getting out of that chair and getting to some food and water.

Within minutes I heard only one set of footsteps coming

my way. My heart started to pound. I didn't know whether it was the man I had come to hate or his companion. I felt someone's hand peeling away the duct tape from my wrists and ankles. Then the blindfold came off and the bandanna was removed from my mouth. I started coughing and I was so weak I couldn't cover my mouth. My body was limp. There was a man, dark skinned like my dad, staring at me. He was more muscular and looked a lot older than my father, though. His hair was cut close to his head, almost bald. He had a light mustache and goatee and he appeared to be well groomed. He didn't look mean like the bad man who had brought me there and for some reason I didn't feel afraid anymore. I actually felt a sense of security, like I had been rescued. He picked me up out of the chair and my back ached terribly. He carried me out of the shack and put me in a dark-colored SUV. It was air-conditioned inside and the soft leather seats felt so comfortable compared to the hard chair I had been sitting in all those days. I lay across the backseat and struggled to keep my eyes open.

"You hungry?" the man asked, climbing into the driver's seat.

I tried to answer him but I couldn't. I was too weak. The man picked up a Kit Kat, opened the wrapper, and handed the four chocolate wafers back to me.

I began eating the Kit Kat like it was a McDonald's cheeseburger. I lifted my head a little when the man pulled up in the parking lot of a fast-food restaurant. I was licking my dirty fingers when he turned off the car and hopped out.

"I'll be right back," he said.

I just nodded real slowly. When he got back inside the car he sat in the backseat beside me. He sat me up and placed a bunch of food in front of me. I reached out for the drink he had in his hand and he put the straw in it and gave it to me. My hands were shaking so badly that I couldn't hold the cup on my own. He had to help me. He fed me, too. After eating the chicken sandwich, French fries, and juice, I burst into tears.

The man rubbed my head, starting from my hairline. He worked his way down to the middle of my back where my ponytail ceased.

"I'm sorry about what you had to go through," he said. "But that's life. Children pay for the sins of their fathers."

Not paying him much attention, I lay back down on the seat and continued crying softly. The man discarded all the trash from the food and then got back in the driver's seat. Flashbacks of what happened to my parents kept piercing my brain. The vivid images, the pleasant breeze that poured in all four of the car windows, and my ongoing tears put me in a deep sleep. When I woke up I was being carried from the car to a house. I was taken upstairs and placed on a bed. I was sweaty and sticky and my clothes were filthy with bloodstains all over them. I was surprised that the man had laid me on clean sheets.

"I'm Chatman, by the way," the man finally introduced himself to me. "Sophia will come clean you up, okay?"

I nodded my head yes.

He turned to walk out of the room and then paused. He looked back at me and assured me, "If you need anything, she's the one to ask, all right?"

I nodded yes again.

Chatman then continued out of the room. He closed the door behind him.

Immediately, I felt myself becoming tired again. My eyes were closing and I was just about asleep when a young yellow-toned girl with tiny eyes and black curly hair came into the room. Unable to control my nerves, I jumped.

She pouted and approached me slowly.

"What's the matter?" she sang in her Asian accent.

"I want my mommy!" I cried out.

The woman, whom I assumed to be Sophia, knelt down by the bedside. Her eyes watered as she reached out and wrapped her skinny arms around me.

"I know, sweetheart," she sang, rubbing my back. "And I'm sure your mommy wants to be with you, too."

Sophia began to take me out of my clothes. She wrapped a towel around me.

"My name is Sophia. What's yours?" she asked, walking me down the hall to the bathroom.

"Sienna," I whispered.

"Sienna? Is that what you said? Don't be shy."

I nodded as she placed me in a tub of warm water.

"That's a pretty name," she commented, dipping a washcloth in the water and wringing it out. She started washing my face, scrubbing my forehead first. Then she put a bar of soap inside the washcloth and began scrubbing my body with it. After she was done, she rinsed me off with the water. Next, she gently laid me backward just enough for my hair to fall in the water. I was resistant, scared to go back, but she sang in her little voice that she was not going to hurt me. She took out my ponytail and wet my hair thoroughly. Then she shampooed it. A few washes later she put conditioner in and combed it through each strand.

"You're hair is so pretty and long. Is your mother's hair like this?" she asked. "I bet she was one pretty lady."

I nodded, almost breaking into tears again envisioning my mother's beautiful lemon-colored skin and long dark hair, her bronze eyes looking down at me and her smile that lit up my life. Sophia wiped away the one tear that managed to escape and asked, "How old are you?"

I held up five little fingers.

"Five? I have a boy your age. Well he's a couple years older actually, but . . ." Sophia paused. "I miss him so much." She sniffled. "I know how you must feel."

After that it was complete silence. Sophia rinsed the conditioner from my hair, took me out of the tub, dried me, and dressed me in a big T-shirt and some mix-match socks. She took me back to the bedroom I would later call my own. She put me in the bed and walked over to close and lock the only window in the room. By then it had grown dark outside. I remember purposely watching her every move. The fact of the matter was I didn't trust her. I didn't trust anyone at that point. I couldn't. For all I knew everybody in the house was out to hurt me. I mean, I had witnessed a man who had smiled in my father's face right before he murdered him. So as far as I was concerned, it was the people who befriended you whom you had to watch close. And that's what I did. I paid close attention to everyone—all the women who came and went, Chatman, and all his workers. And in the process I learned a lot.

I learned all about Chatman's business in the sex trade, the boatloads—or shipments as he called them—of women from overseas he would pay for, the doctors that would come to the house to examine them in the basement, and the circle of guys Chatman had working for him that would do anything he asked at the drop of a hat. I learned that Chatman had power and along with his power came money. And in just two short years I watched Chatman go from a small-time businessman who had a three-bedroom home in a rough part of Florida to a self-made billionaire who laid down cash for a fifteen-thousand-square-foot mansion in an affluent neighborhood in Miami Beach called Star Island.

It was a Tuesday when we moved into the ten-bedroom, nine-and-a-half-bathroom mansion. I remember because it was the day of the last episode of *Encyclopedia Brown* and I had to miss it because we hadn't gotten the cable connected yet. Sophia was most excited about the move. From the day that Chatman came home with pictures of the new house until months later when we were actually able to move into it, she spent the hours she was supposed to use home-schooling me expressing how happy she would be once Chatman moved us out of the small house and into the huge dream home. She had big plans for that house and had no idea that she'd never step foot in it. Apparently she and Chatman had totally different agendas. I will never forget it.

A U-haul truck pulled up to our house. We all thought it was there to move all the things we had packed up. But as it turned out, it was there to take away the women Chatman made his fortune off of over the past decade, among them Sophia. I was in Sophia's room playing in her makeup when we both got wind of the news. One of the other Thai girls came in crying. Sophia, nurturing as she was, rushed to console her.

"Noi, what's wrong?" Sophia asked her, rubbing her back.

"He's selling us!" Noi wept.

"He's what?" Sophia asked.

"He's selling us. Our time is up. He's getting new women, younger ones. We're not going with him. He's sending us away."

Sophia grew concerned. "Where did you hear this?"

"From his mouth! That U-haul out there isn't for this furniture! It's for us!" Noi screamed.

Anger took hold of Sophia's face as she let the information penetrate. Then she got up from the bed and walked out the room. I jumped from the vanity and followed behind her, only I stopped in the hall when she barged into Chatman's office.

"Chatman, tell me you're not getting rid of us!" she demanded right away.

"Now is not the time, Sophia," I heard Chatman say in an oddly calm tone.

I couldn't see Chatman, but I could imagine the look on his face. Over the years I had gotten to know Chatman and based on what I knew I wouldn't have dared do what Sophia had. It was a wonder she was still standing. The Chatman I knew would have slapped her into the kitchen the minute he realized it was she who had swung his office door open.

"Now is the time, Chatman! I've been with you since I was fifteen years old! That's ten years, Chatman! You didn't do this alone! You've achieved all that you have on our hard work! We planted the seeds and you mean to tell me you're not even going to let us taste the fruit! You're gonna replace us with some girls who didn't contribute one second to the last ten years that we all spent building your so-called empire!" Sophia ranted.

"*I said, now is not the time, Sophia!*" Chatman yelled.

At that point, I backed into Sophia's room, only peeking out her doorway. Noi stood in front of me and some of the other girls were scattered in the hall whispering among themselves.

"Chatman!" Sophia shouted one last time before being slapped off her feet.

Next thing I knew, her frail body flew out of Chatman's office and onto the hallway floor. A.J., Chatman's right hand, immediately started running up the steps from downstairs.

"What's going on, boss?" A.J. asked in a ready-for-action tone.

"What did you just call me?" Chatman asked A.J.

A.J. looked baffled. "Boss," he repeated himself.

"Say it louder," Chatman ordered, looking down at Sophia cringing in fear on the floor.

"Boss!" A.J. shouted, following Chatman's instructions.

"You hear that, bitch! I'm the boss around this motherfucka!" Chatman said, kicking Sophia in her stomach and ribs.

Sobbing, Sophia cowered beneath Chatman, who was beating her to no end. A.J. tried to get Chatman to let up off of Sophia several times before he actually did, and by then she was covered in blood and could hardly walk. "Take the bitch to the truck!" Chatman instructed A.J. "Y'all other bitches follow!" he yelled to the other girls who were all in the hallway crying in dismay.

"What about my boy, Chatman? Huh? Is that deal off, too?" Sophia whimpered as she was being carried down the steps by A.J.

"Shut the fuck up," A.J. told her as more of a warning than a command.

But she kept going. "You promised me! You promised him! Please! Please send for my boy like you promised!"

Chatman leaned over the banister to respond to Sophia. "You act like you've been a fucking angel through this! You got knocked up the day you got here! The only reason why I didn't beat that baby out of you was because you kept the pregnancy from me!"

"I was fifteen years old! I hardly spoke English then! If you wanna blame somebody, blame your fucking partner! He sought me out!" Sophia sobbed.

"That's why he's not here anymore!" Chatman retorted. "And now you won't be here anymore! I can start fresh and run my business the way it's meant to be run without dis̶ you! Every time I turn my back you're in one faces! A.J., get her the fuck out of here!"

A.J. headed for the front door, carrying Sophı̶ in his arms.

"Oh, and as for your son, I'll send for him, all right! He'll follow in his mother's and his father's footsteps! He'll work for me and I'ma use 'im up 'til he can't be used no more, then throw 'im over like I did his scheming, conniving, worthless parents!"

"You're a cruel bastard, Chatman! And I hope you burn in the hottest pits of hell!" were the last words I heard Sophia speak.

I was seven at the time and a child no more. I had seen so much in my short life that my mind and my heart had long outgrown my body. I was all alone once again, taken away from a person whom I had considered to be another mother. It was weird that I didn't cry, though. I just remember thinking that I had to be tough. I remember telling myself that I was a woman now and that I was left to teach myself, to understand, and to deal with the world I had been given. I made myself a promise that from that day on I would not get attached to anyone ever again, man, woman, or child.

That promise was easy to keep even when we moved into the mansion and the new boatload of more than twenty teenage girls moved in with us. Chatman had given me my own room and that's where I stayed most of the time, playing with my dolls or using Sophia's home-schooling material to teach myself stuff like reading and mathematics.

I didn't communicate with the new girls. Most of them didn't speak English well anyway. So for a long time I stayed to myself, until another newcomer drew me out of my shell.

One afternoon, Chatman had left the house with A.J. and when they returned they had a boy with them. He was older than me but much younger than any of Chatman's workers. Chatman called me into his office and introduced me to the boy.

"Sienna, this is Ryan," Chatman said.

Then he told me that Ryan would be staying with us for a while and that I was to share my room with him. I wasn't thrilled about having to share my room, but for some reason I felt an instant connection to Ryan, so I didn't complain. I just told Chatman okay and walked Ryan out of Chatman's office and down the long marble hallway to my room.

"How old are you?" I asked Ryan as soon as we got in my room. I sat down on my bed and he stood in the middle of the floor as if he was lost.

"Nine," he said, looking around. "How old are you?"

"Seven and a half. Where are you from?" I continued my personal questionnaire.

"This is a big house," Ryan said, looking up at the ceiling. "Is your dad rich?" he asked.

"My dad is dead," I answered him.

He took his eyes off the ceiling and looked at me. His big brown eyes softened and buck teeth bit his bottom lip.

"Your dad is dead, too?" he asked.

I nodded my head. "So where are you from, like I said?"

"Thailand," he responded. "Where you from?"

"Here. But my mom is in the Dominican Republic," I said, remembering what the man who killed my father had told Chatman. "And one day I'm going to find her and live with her."

"My mom is here in America," he said. "She used to live

here. Do you know her?" He pulled out a small cut-off picture of a beautiful lady and put it in my face.

"That's Sophia," I said, enthused. "I know her. She took care of me."

"She did?" he asked, surprised.

"Uh-huh."

"Do you know where she is now?" he asked.

"No," I said, wanting to change the topic.

"I want to find my mom, too," he said, looking down at the picture.

Feeling sadness coming on, I quickly turned chipper and suggested, "You can help me find my mom and I can help you find yours." I figured I'd offer hope.

"Okay," he said, nodding his head as if he were in negotiations.

I just smiled at the little naïve boy and then introduced him to my toys. I took a pretty sudden liking to Ryan. I guessed it was because we had similar situations and goals and we often shared them with each other. He became the only person in the house I truly trusted and confided in and over time we found ourselves dangerously attracted to each other. But who knew the chemistry that brewed between us would turn out to be fire and ice.

CHAPTER 2

"Make a wish and blow out your candles!" Chatman's wheezing voice sounded over the chatter in the bistro.

I closed my eyes and whispered silently, *I wish to see my mom again.*

Then I blew on the cake as hard as I could. Everybody clapped and cheered. The waitress cut the cake and started handing pieces out to everybody. Of course, I got my slice first and it was the biggest. The whole crown off my princess cake belonged to me. Ryan got the lips and everybody else got whatever they were given. They were adults anyway so it didn't matter to them. Ryan and I were the only two people at my tenth birthday party who were under eighteen.

We all lounged in Lea's Tea Room and Bistro and ate the cake and ice cream, occasionally laughing at the different people who would walk up and tug on the restaurant's doors.

They would often try again and again until the hostess would tell them that the restaurant was closed due to a private party.

When we were done, Chatman paid the bill and we left. Ryan and I rode in the backseat of Chatman's Rolls-Royce Silver Spur. A.J. and another one of Chatman's workers got into A.J.'s Porsche 911. Samantha, Chatman's new top lady, drove three other women in her Jaguar XJ6. I remember the stunned look on people's faces as we pulled out of the parking garage of the Bal Harbour Shops in a line of brand-new luxury vehicles. It made me feel important, like I was a movie star. And from that moment on I knew what I wanted to be when I grew up.

Back at the house everybody retreated to their bedrooms except for Chatman, A.J., and the other guys. They went into the game room to play pool. They even invited Ryan in there with them. I was on my way to my room when Samantha called me to her room, which was one of the four master suites in the house, the other three being occupied by Chatman, A.J. and Chatman's office. She had it decorated in pink and gold with luxurious satin bedding and thick velvet drapes. She was changing into her pajamas when I got there. I sat on her big canopy bed and watched her, studying her body language and her elegant movements.

There was something about Samantha that made her stand out from the other women. She was so graceful and she had beauty inside and out. I guess that was why she had made it to the top. I mean, she had come to the house along with twenty-four other women three years ago, and they all started from the same spot. But Samantha had managed to get her own suite, her own car, and privileges that the other women were still hoping for, like going shopping without a chaperone.

I could tell that the other women were jealous of her. They

tended to leave Samantha out of their cliques. But Samantha was their boss in a way—well, more like their supervisor—so if they were smart they would try to be on her good side. They would stay around her and learn from her, like I did. I admired her.

"So, how does it feel to be ten?" she asked me.

"Good, I guess."

"You're in the two digits now," she said, removing her pearl necklace from around her neck. "I remember when I was ten. I was living in Panama with my family. It was twelve of us in a one-bedroom. We all worked, even my younger brothers and sisters. We all had to help out," she said, turning toward me. "You got it good, little lady."

"You had a job when you were ten?" I asked, surprised.

"Actually, I had a job when I was six. I used to walk the streets and shine people's shoes. Or sometimes I would sell flowers or candy. By the time I was ten I was working on a sugarcane plantation."

"So, your mom and dad didn't take care of you?" I asked.

"My mom and dad couldn't afford to take care of us on their own salaries. It would not have been enough for us all. See, that's why I say you have it good. In my country, kids don't live like this," she said, opening her arms as if to tell me to look around.

"Is that why you came here to the United States?"

"I wouldn't say I 'came here,'" Samantha said, wrapping herself in her bathrobe. She sat down beside me on the bed and continued, "That would sound voluntary. I was forced to come here. My parents sold me to a man back in my country when I was twelve. It got really bad for them and they had a lot of debt. The man they sold me to promised them he would send me to school in America and that all I had to do in return was work in his factory when I was finished. My parents were grateful to him. They bowed down to him the day they sold me as if he was God. I'll never forget that. I was so upset and so afraid and yet they were so happy and so relieved.

"The man never sent me to school. Instead, he immediately put me to work. I worked for him for four years and in that time I learned the business. And that's what ultimately saved me. That's what kept me from following the path of most of the girls who are in this industry. A lot of them end up killing themselves or self-medicating because it's just hard to deal with everything, from being sold by your own parents and then forced to do things that you don't understand and feeling like there is absolutely no help or no hope for you. It can drive a person crazy. But I saw everything differently. I saw the money and the opportunities that came from making the money. And I decided that if I was going to survive, I had to make money and therefore create opportunities for myself. And that's what I did. I worked and although it disgusted me and I hated it, I trained myself to be good at it. I increased my value and instead of being used as trash like most girls and women in the trade, I became treasure. That's what attracted Chatman to me, which is how I ended up here in America."

"So after all these years, don't you miss your mom and dad?" I asked, trying to get answers about how to handle the emptiness I felt from not having my parents.

Samantha's eyebrows rose. "Yeah, I do. I miss my whole family, but . . ."

"But what?" I inquired.

"It's like you start all over. You get new families. You get new loved ones. Your whole life changes. Like how I'm Samantha now."

"What do you mean?"

She smirked and responded, "My mom didn't name me Samantha. My birth name was Marta. Then the man who bought me first named me Maria and then when I came here Chatman named me Samantha."

"Why did they change your name?" I inquired.

"It's a way of detaching you from your past. It's how they keep control. But you don't have to worry about that. Your mother named you Sienna, right?"

I nodded.

"Well, if Chatman hasn't changed your name by now then he doesn't have plans to. So you'll be Sienna forever." Samantha smiled.

"Is Chatman going to sell you one day?"

"I don't know," she said, shrugging her shoulders. "Only time will tell. But I know I'm going to work hard so that he won't. Chatman's pretty cool, you know. As long as you stay in line, do what he says, and make him some money, he won't give you problems. Besides, this here beats Panama by a long shot. I'm hoping to become a citizen one day so I can stay here." Samantha stretched out her tanned arms and started tickling me, reminding me of how my father used to tickle me all the time. "I'm trying to be an American like you, Sienna. Only here does a girl get so many lavish gifts for her tenth birthday," she said, chuckling. Then she stopped tickling me and sat up. "I remember the first birthday you had while I was living here. You were what, seven?" she asked.

I squinted my eyes and looked up at the ceiling, still smiling from the laughter she had caused me. "Yup."

"Yeah, 'cause that's when you got that seven-hundred-dollar cashier's check from Chatman. Then when you were eight you got to take whoever you wanted with you on that cruise to the Bahamas. And what was it last year? Oh yeah, the mink jacket and the diamond earrings. And we're not even going to talk about today. You must have spent what, five thousand, six thousand dollars in Bal Harbour? And Chatman had them shut down the entire tea room so that we could use just a small corner of it to celebrate your birthday. Little lady, you are spoiled rotten," she summed up.

Then she reached in the pocket of her bathrobe and pulled out a small gift-wrapped box. "As if you don't have enough already, this is for you," Samantha said, extending the box to me.

I was surprised. I snatched the gift and anxiously tore open the bright purple wrapping paper. When I opened the box there was a tiny frame inside. As I was picking up the frame to get a good look at the picture that was in it, Samantha began explaining.

"It's a picture of your mother," she said, her words making my heart skip beats.

I gazed at the tiny, dated photo. And indeed it was my mom. I didn't know what to say or how to react. My first thought was that Samantha knew my mom and that maybe my mom would come walking through her bedroom door shouting, "Surprise!"

"It's from Chatman. He knows how much you miss your mother and he wanted you to have her picture so that you could see her every day. He wanted me to let you know, too, that he went through a lot to get it."

I can't explain how I felt at that moment. Instantly, I bombarded Samantha with questions about my mom's whereabouts and whether Chatman could take me to her. But in the end, when I realized that I wouldn't get that opportunity, I was just happy to have a picture of her. I hugged Samantha tight and thanked her.

"Don't thank me, thank Chatman," she said.

I jumped off her bed to do just that and she reached out and grabbed my wrist.

"Hey," she said. "Chatman sees something in you. You're young so you won't understand this, but, out of all us girls here, you're the one little lady. You're the one who's gonna make the difference."

Samantha was right; I didn't understand what she had told me. First of all, I was in a hurry to go give Chatman a huge hug and kiss. Second, I wanted to show Ryan the picture of my mom. So I just smiled at Samantha as if I knew what she meant and darted out of her room.

"Chatman! Chatman!" I shouted gleefully. I ran down the wide spiral staircase and into the game room.

The guys had all paused what they were doing and looked in my direction. I ran to Chatman and wrapped my arms around his waist. I buried my head in his stomach and closed my eyes, trying to stop the tears that I felt emerging.

"Chatman, thank you so much for giving me this picture of my mom. This is the best birthday gift ever!" I told him, squeezing him.

Chatman hugged me back and said, "Your welcome, baby. You see what happens when you're a good girl?"

I nodded my head up and down and I couldn't stop smiling. I released Chatman and walked over to Ryan, pride in every step.

"Look. Isn't she pretty?" I asked, holding the frame up to his eyes. He reached out to hold it but I didn't give it to him.

"Yeah, I guess so," Ryan said bashfully.

Then A.J. butted in and said, "Aww, go ahead and say yeah. If she's pretty, she's pretty. There's nothing wrong with a man thinking that a woman is pretty."

Ryan looked at me and I looked at him. Then I blushed.

"All right, all right," Chatman broke the tension. "Go back upstairs and get settled for bed."

I said good night to Chatman and the guys and I went to my room. I put on my pajamas and brushed my teeth, all while still holding on to my mom's picture. Right before I got in bed, I knelt down to pray. I thanked God for granting my birthday wish and allowing me to see my mom again. Even though she wasn't physically here, it was good enough, and it taught me that my wishes could come true.

It was a rainy morning. Chatman left early for a business meeting. A.J. was supposed to be watching Ryan and me, but he had fallen asleep on the couch in the family room.

"I'm bored," I whispered to Ryan, who was sitting on the opposite side of the sectional as me.

"Me, too," he whispered back.

"Let's play something," I suggested.

"What?"

"I don't know. Hide-and-go-seek."

Ryan's eyes lit up. We used to play hide-and-go-seek a lot when we were younger. But as we got older it became more of a game of catch a girl freak a girl.

Grinning, he said, "All right."

I held my finger to my mouth, gesturing for Ryan to be quiet. We both stood up from the couch slowly, freezing whenever A.J. moved. Once off the couch, we tiptoed out of the family room. We headed for the huge staircase, Ryan going up one side and me the other. When we got to the second floor, we giggled at our sneakiness.

"Put your foot in," I instructed Ryan, putting my right foot forward.

"My momma and ya momma were hanging up clothes. My momma punched ya momma right dead in the nose. What color was the blood?" I recited as I pointed to my foot and Ryan's to the rhythm of the song.

"Red. R-e-d. Okay, I'm it," I said, pointing to my foot. "Go hide, punk," I teased.

Ryan took off as I stood with my face against the wall in the hallway. Covering my eyes with my hands I counted to twenty slowly. When I was done, I darted toward my room. I knew where to look for Ryan because he tended to hide in the same places all the time. I looked under my bed and under my blankets. I looked in my closet then behind the door. I looked behind the dressers and the drapes. Ryan was not in there, which was surprising. He was usually in one of those places and he was always in my room. I ran back out into the hallway and down to Ryan's room.

I searched everywhere, under his bed, in his closet, and behind everything that moved. No Ryan. I was really shocked. It never took me long to find Ryan. He was not good at hiding. I decided to go back to my room. But instead of looking around, I figured I would be slick. I stood at the doorway for a while without making a move or a sound. And just as I guessed he would, Ryan slowly and quietly peeped his head out of my clothes hamper.

"Ahhh! I got you!" I shouted, running over to him and tapping his head.

I darted out of the room and Ryan was right behind me. But I was able to tag the base before him and therefore he was it. It was my turn to hide and his turn to seek.

Ryan was bent over with his hands on his knees against the wall in the hallway. He was trying to catch his breath.

"You ready?" I asked him, eager to get in my hiding spot.

He shook his head and stood up, turning to face the wall. He put his hands over his eyes and I took off.

"One, two, three, four, five . . . " he counted.

I ran to my room first, purposely making noise along the way, and I closed my bedroom door. I wanted to fake Ryan out and have him think I went in there. Then I walked back past Ryan to go in Chatman's office. I had the perfect hiding place in mind. There was a door in the ceiling in Chatman's office that I always wondered about. I didn't think anyone noticed it because it was painted to blend well with the ceiling. I figured Ryan would never find me in there and I would be the hide-and-seek champion.

I climbed up on Chatman's desk and pulled the string that hung from the secret door. A small staircase was revealed and I climbed up and realized I was just in the attic. I never would have thought it was just the attic. I mean, I had been in the attic plenty of times before. There is another entrance in the ceiling in the hallway near my room. I had to put some of my toys and old clothes up there over the years. Disappointed that my discovery wasn't really a discovery at all, I started to climb back down the stairs and hide someplace else. But Ryan's voice shouting "Ready or not here I come" made me stay put. I pulled the stairs back up and closed myself in the attic. I waited anxiously for Ryan to search the entire second floor before he would yell, "I give up." I had gotten the urge to pee and everything but I wasn't going to give up that hiding space. I heard him running up and down the hall. I heard different doors opening and closing. I laughed at the thought of Ryan looking for me everywhere possible and coming up short each time.

Then, just as I was anticipating Ryan saying the magic words and me being crowned champion, I heard Chatman's voice. I grew stiff, trying to think of a way out of his office without being caught. Chatman forbade anyone from being in his office without his permission. There was no telling what he would have done to me had he found out that I had ignored his golden rule. I started to hurry up and climb out, but I heard his footsteps approaching. Then I figured I would just crawl through the attic to the other door that was in the hallway, but there were so many boxes and bags in the way that I couldn't—not without making a ruckus anyway.

"Ryan, where's Sienna?" Chatman's raspy voice asked.

"In her room," he guessed.

"A.J.!" Chatman yelled. "Get up!"

I heard Chatman enter his office and I got goose bumps. I'd never gotten in serious trouble with him before, but I had seen others do so and the consequences were something I didn't want any parts of.

"You can sit down," Chatman told somebody, then he yelled out, "Ryan, come here!"

From what I heard, Ryan and A.J. both entered the office at the same time and Chatman instructed them to sit down as well.

"I have a bit of a situation on my hands concerning our next shipment. Now, the connect I had with the coast guard is going up on me tremendously. I mean, at first, he was taking his share up by one percent each deal. Then we had agreed upon stopping it after the sixth deal. Meaning that the first deal we did he charged me a set fee, then the second deal it would increase by one percent and the third deal by one more percent and so forth and so on until the sixth deal. After that it would be the same fee every time.

"Well, at our last meeting he told me that he wasn't stopping the percentage and in fact he was going up two percent each deal from here on out."

"You serious?" A.J.'s voice asked, irritated. "Yo, just gimme the word."

"You know what it is?" Chatman asked rhetorically. "It's all the shit that's been happening. First it was the cocaine cowboys. Now it's these damn cartels. These motherfuckers got everybody hot right now. So the connect is taxing the hell out of me."

"Damn, that's fucked up," A.J. said.

"But everything happens for a reason, you know. They have too many people's eyes on them. We don't need the heat. What we do is so off the radar right now that it would be stupid to turn any heads our way. We just have to find another source of transpo and that's why I brought my man Sammy here today."

"What's up?" A.J. apparently greeted the man.

I finally heard the man's voice. "How's it goin'?"

"Sammy does passports, birth certificates, IDs, Social Security cards, everything. With him on our team, we'll be able to start flyin' shipments in, which is better because it's cheaper, faster, and less risky," Chatman said before pausing. Then he continued, "You figure I can have five women per flight on an average of ten flights a day per airline. Dealing with five airlines, that's about two hundred fifty women every day. In thirty days that's seventy-five hundred women!" Chatman grew excited.

"Hell yeah." A.J.'s excitement grew as well. "Shit, we was doing about three hundred every two-three years. You talkin' about twenty-five times that in one fuckin' month!"

"Crazy, right?" Chatman asked.

"Crazy? Niggas, that's astronomical. Why we ain't been think of this shit?"

"First of all we was used to doing things one way. It's the way my uncle taught me and the way I taught y'all. Second, we ain't have Sammy here."

"I'm wit' it, baby," A.J. said. "Let's get this shit crackin', like, today! You know how much money we talkin'?"

"All right, so the way we'll do it is, I'll have my translator communicating with the sellers to get the names, ages, and description of each body. Then the translator will type it all up and hand it over to you, Ryan. You will then file it away in the travelers' briefcase and I'll show you how. Then Sammy, you'll basically pick up the briefcase each month. You do all the documents and file everything back in the briefcase and return it to Ryan. Ryan, you will then put the briefcase in here and I'll show you where. You think you can handle that?"

I was up in the attic listening for Ryan's response. I was shocked that Chatman had brought him in on a business meeting and then actually given him a role. That made me jealous in a way. My competitive side had me thinking that I should have been offered a role before Ryan. I had been there the longest and as far as I was concerned, I was smarter than him.

"Yeah," Ryan said with somewhat of a shaky tone.

"You sure? Because this is a very important job and if you don't think you can handle it, let me know, I'll give it to somebody else. I just figured you were old enough now to start earning your stay around here, you know what I mean?"

Ryan must have nodded yes because I heard nothing. Chatman continued on as if Ryan had accepted the position.

"Now, A.J., you'll be coordinating the flying arrangements,

the flights, times, departures, and arrivals. You'll make sure everyone arrives at the same time so we'll only have to make one trip. I'll have somebody do the pickups, probably Jim."

"I don't mean to interrupt," Sammy's voice sounded, "but you're gonna want more than one guy to do your pickups. You're gonna want a few guys in different vehicles. You don't wanna show up and pile them all in one big van. That will look suspicious."

"Yeah, yeah, I know. I have a meeting with one of the shuttle bus drivers who does routes at the airport. You know those ones that take people to the parking lot?"

"Ohhh, that would be perfect," Sammy said.

"So, I have it pretty much mapped out. It's just a few things I have to tie up with the coast guard and then I can say we're good to go."

"What has to be tied up with them?" A.J. asked.

"I don't want to just stop doing shipments with them cold turkey. They're hurting right now. They need my money. Now, I can easily say that I can't afford the price increase. But if they notice that my shipments stop and my business keeps going they may try some slick stuff and expose me. That's why you have to be really careful who you do business with because the minute shit goes south niggas is lookin' for their scapegoat. You know a nigga'll whistle quick to avoid jail time."

"Shit, that's why it's better to knock niggas off sometimes."

"It's not so simple. You got the feds, the DEA, the ATF, everybody trying to make a name for themselves. We can't just pluck off a coast guard member without causing uproar. We can't afford that time. It's too much money to be made."

"I feel you."

"So, I'll just let the connects know that business is slow and

I'll schedule a shipment with them as soon as things pick up. That way, it's no bad blood between us and if we ever need to use them again, which we probably will, that bridge won't be burned."

"Well, I'm following your lead," A.J. said.

"So, meeting adjourned, then?"

"Meeting adjourned," A.J. said.

"Sounds good to me," Sammy said.

Then after a brief silence, I heard Chatman say, "Look at this! This shit looks official like a motherfucker!"

"Oh hell yeah, boss," A.J. agreed.

I figured they were looking at samples of Sammy's work. I wished I could have seen. But having heard all that I did was efficient enough. I learned a lot up there in the attic—a lot that didn't necessarily do me any good at that time, but definitely helped me down the road.

"Welcome to the team," Chatman told Sammy, I assumed. Then I heard Chatman get up out of his chair and the guys left the office. Chatman closed his office door and that was my cue. I quietly opened the attic door and climbed down the staircase. I stepped onto Chatman's desk and closed the attic door, then stepped down onto the floor and opened the office door slightly. I peered out into the hall and saw no one. I heard the front door opening and I slipped out the office, closing the door behind me. I went in my room and sat on my bed. I smiled slyly, feeling like I had just gotten away with murder.

CHAPTER 3

"*Fuck bitches, get money...*" "Turn that up!" I instructed Ryan, who was stretched out across my bed flipping through the pages of a *Source* magazine with Tupac on the cover. I bopped my head and poked out my lips, reciting the lyrics to my favorite Junior M.A.F.I.A. song. Standing in front of the mirror, I was removing the rollers from my hair, getting ready to go out. It was spring break, and not only that, I had just become a teenager. So I was planning to party hard. I applied my eyeliner and mascara and then my lipstick. I was determined to pass for at least eighteen. Being five-foot-seven with the physique of a supermodel, I was sure I could pull it off.

"Yo, where do you think you are going?" Ryan finally closed the magazine and placed his eyes on me.

"I don't know. Crobar or somewhere. I might just walk up and down Ocean Drive. It's spring break! You know how many people are going to be out? You know how many parties it's going to be?"

Ryan laughed, revealing those two buck teeth he'd never fully grown into.

"What's so funny?"

"You really think Chatman is goin' let you out the house lookin' like that to go walk up and down South Beach?"

I rolled my eyes and in a grown-up voice, I told him, "I am a grown woman. Chatman doesn't have to know my every move anymore."

Ryan laughed even louder. "So you sayin' you gonna sneak out?"

"Those were your words, not mine," I said with a devilish grin.

"By yourself?" Ryan asked further.

"Unless you're coming with me," I answered him.

"Naw, not me. I just got a promotion. I ain't tryin' to lose it."

"Oh, please, errand boy! All you do is run around fetching stuff for everybody! How hard will it be to say good-bye to that?!" I teased.

"It's not about the now, stupid. It's about the later. If I show Chatman that I can be trusted doing the small things, eventually he will move me up to the big things," Ryan theorized.

"Well I say, by the time Chatman decides to move you up to the quote-unquote 'big things,' you going out with me tonight will be long forgotten."

Ryan shook his head after giving what I said some thought. "Naw. People like Chatman don't forget stuff."

I sucked my teeth. "Okay, well, let's say that Chatman never finds out. Then it won't be anything for either of us to worry about, will it?"

"Chatman finds out everything," Ryan maintained his position.

"Oh my God! You are like Chatman's spokesperson or something! Get off his you know what!" I teased him some more. "How old are you?"

"Fifteen," Ryan said, straightening his face. "You know that."

"Yeah well, at what age do boys normally grow balls?"

Ryan laughed again, covering his head with the magazine he had been reading. "Aw man, you comin' dead at me."

"I'm just curious," I said, keeping a straight face.

After a lot of teasing and convincing I finally got Ryan to sneak out with me. I had it all mapped out. Chatman usually checked in on Ryan and me before he went to bed each night, which was normally around two in the morning, after the last escort for the day returned home. So the way I figured it, as long as we were tucked in bed by a quarter to two then we would be safe. It was close to nine when we both were freshened up and ready to go. Our keys and some cash from Samantha in hand, we assisted each other in climbing out through the kitchen window.

It was such a nice March night, perfect for walking. I joked to Ryan that if only I was licensed I would have stolen Chatman's boat to take us to the action. He found it funny but said he believed me. We walked from the exclusive island that housed our mansion and made our way to MacArthur Causeway, but not before first cleverly sneaking past the twenty-four-hour security post. Once on Route 41 we were able to get to Fifth Street and then to Collins Avenue. From there we were home free. Ryan and I took a cab to Ocean Drive and just as I had imagined, it was packed. We didn't need to get in any of the clubs to have a good time. We could have easily had as much fun walking up and down the strip.

When we got out of the cab, we didn't know which way to go. Ryan's eyes lit up like a Christmas tree, looking at all the people and the sights. This was our first time in the midst of Miami's nightlife and it happened to be during the most anticipated and crowded week of all. We both were taken aback, a bit nervous even. Surrounded by the herd of older, bigger, drunken men and women, Ryan and I were like guppies in a pool of sharks. It was so rowdy. Girls went topless while guys fondled them. I didn't know if I was cut out for that scene. I sensed danger as guys gawked at me. I wasn't sure if they would try to rip my clothes off or what. Ryan didn't say much, but I could tell he was uncomfortable by how tightly he held my hand. It wasn't until we got off the street that we loosened up and blended in with the crowd.

After a couple of hours we found ourselves taking shots of tequila in a small bar off Washington Avenue. The other drinkers were cheering us on. I was having the time of my life, feeling liberated. I had been cooped up in the house under Chatman's watch for far too long. The way I saw it, it was time for me to experience the outside world. Ryan was enjoying himself, too, I could tell, although he was taking fewer shots than me and carrying himself more modestly than I was. We danced to a few of the popular songs and we lost ourselves in the music, at times feeling on each other as if we were lovers rather than friends. The time had escaped us and we didn't wind up leaving the bar until it had closed at two-thirty.

When Ryan and I got home, neither of us wanted to go inside. We were scared that the alarm would sound and give us up. We tried to get Samantha's attention by throwing rocks at the window of her bedroom, but with no success. We contemplated disabling the alarm from the keypad but, even though it wouldn't make as much noise as the alarm going off, there was a possibility that the minor beep would wake Chatman. We tried going around the back of the house and sleeping inside the pool house. The door was locked. Walking back to the main entry, we heard a whisper.

"Hurry up!" Samantha was standing in the doorway waving us toward her.

We jogged over to her in relief.

"You two are way late," she said softly, shooing us in.

"Sorry." I giggled, still a bit intoxicated.

Ryan walked me to my room and saw me to bed and then he disappeared. I changed into my pajamas and slipped under my covers. My night had ended beautifully, but at the expense of the morning to follow.

"Where's Samantha?" I shouted upon seeing Samantha's room emptied of her belongings. I had plans on thanking her for covering up for Ryan and me, but she was gone and it was just past ten in the morning. That was unusual in that house. Everybody slept until at least eleven.

Then Ryan appeared in the hallway. We looked at each other grimly, mentally concluding that Chatman had found out about Samantha being an accomplice to our escapade and her abrupt absence was the consequence. Chatman never confirmed why Samantha had left or if her leaving was voluntary or not, but Ryan and I figured our assumptions were correct. It was like I had been stabbed in the heart once again, and in the same spot. Despite the promise I made to myself about getting attached to people, especially in the house, I had grown close to Samantha over the last six years. And for her to have been sent away on account of something stupid I'd done really hurt. I knew how bad she wanted to stay there with Chatman. I knew that she never wanted to be sold again, yet I'd caused it to happen. The whole situation messed me up. And I bet Chatman thought it would teach me not to sneak out again, but all it really did was make me want to sneak out more.

Ryan and I became regulars in Miami's hottest nightclubs. It had gotten to the point where we knew club owners and bartenders on a first-name basis. I was known as Si-Si and Ryan was R.P., his first and middle initials. It was hard at first because after the spring break crowd had returned to college, the club and bar owners were stricter about carding people. But I had something up my sleeve to fix that. I snuck on Chatman's computer and typed up a profile of Ryan and me. I had Ryan put the profiles in the briefcase he had to give to Sammy. Mind you, Sammy was the guy Chatman had hired to create fake passports, birth certificates, and licenses for the illegal aliens Chatman had working for him. Ryan and I had fake IDs in no time.

After that, all we had to do was perfect our plan for sneaking back in the house, which was easy as long as we were home before Chatman went to bed. And Ryan was good at making sure of that. He hardly drank when we went out and he looked at his watch every hour on the hour. So we never got caught again after the first time. No thanks to me, though. My theory was I'd better have as much fun as I could while I was out because when I got home there's no telling what kind of trouble I'd be in. I was the wild one—drinking and clubbing every weekend and sleeping in during the week. There had been a few occasions where I'd even begged Ryan to go out with me on a weekday. He didn't like to, but he wasn't going to see me go anywhere alone. If anything, he would be my chaperone.

Chatman never suspected anything, either. He was so busy selling women, he had no time for us kids. And we didn't mind because we had no time for him. I know I didn't. All I wanted to do over the next two years was hang out, shop, and party. I would smoke some weed every now and then and have a couple of drinks. Ryan often told me I was moving too fast, that I should chill out. But I never listened to "Daddy," a nickname I called him whenever he would lecture me. He always wanted to be a Goody Two-shoes and boring as all hell. I don't think to this day he would have seen the inside of a club if it weren't for me. I didn't blame him, though. I actually thought it was kind of cute. It did something for me that his quirky, odd, Asian looks didn't.

Anyway, I was growing up fast. And some would say before my time. The other women in the house would even tell me I was heading in the wrong direction, but really, what did they know? Most of them hardly spoke English. So I ignored them the way I did Ryan. I convinced myself that I was only having fun and that if Chatman ever felt I was too much to handle he could send me to the Dominican Republic with my mother. That was all I wanted anyhow. In fact, the way I saw it, Chatman's house was always just a place for me to pass the time until I was old enough and smart enough to make my way to my mother's country.

My goal was to find her and live with her. I didn't care if she was poor, either. I just wanted to be with her. So while everybody was scared that Chatman was going to find out about my so-called reckless behavior, I was hoping that he would. They didn't understand that it wasn't my plan to stay with Chatman forever. I had no intention of working for him. Please, I wanted to be a movie star, not a porn star. I knew where I was headed and it was exactly where I wanted to be, so all the constructive criticism and advice that people tried to give me went in one ear and out the other. As far as I was concerned, I was on the right path. I had a plan and I had spent the last two years working toward achieving it. I was either going to run away or get sent away. And since Ryan kept me from the latter, the time was approaching for me to run.

CHAPTER 4

*W*eeks after my fifteenth birthday, I started packing my things. I would pack a little at a time so I wouldn't create suspicion, and whatever I packed I hid in the attic. I knew Chatman hardly went in the attic and if he did happen to go in there all he would see was bags of my clothes, which I was prepared to justify. *I've always stored my old clothes in the attic. You were the one who told me to do that.* I must say, I had become a master manipulator and scheme artist living with Chatman for over a decade.

Everything was unfolding the way I had planned. I was able to pull up information on the Internet about the Dominican Republic. I even tracked down addresses and telephone numbers of people who shared my last name. There being so few Gearases listed, I was sure I had located my relatives. The only thing was I couldn't make international calls from Chatman's. But my plan was to use some of the money I had saved to buy a calling card and call them several days before I would actually leave.

I didn't tell Ryan of my plan. I didn't know if I could trust him to keep it between us. It wasn't that I thought he was slimy like that, but I knew that he wouldn't have wanted me to go and would have probably done anything to get me to stay, including telling Chatman. I wouldn't have been able to blame him either because we had gotten so close, I would have done anything to keep him from running away too if the tables were turned. I don't know what I would have done all those years without Ryan in the house with me. I would have probably died of loneliness. I was grateful for him and I felt bad about leaving him, but seeing my mom again was my top priority. I had prepared myself to the fullest and was just about ready to make my move when an early morning talk with Chatman shattered it all.

"Sienna, wake up." Chatman's voice interrupted my sleep. "We have to talk."

I stretched and moaned and mustered the strength to sit up in my bed. It was just after eight o'clock. Chatman didn't look happy standing before me. In fact, he looked upset. I guessed that he had somehow discovered my plan to leave. I was thinking of something to say, an excuse, an explanation, an apology—something. My mind was blank, though, so I just kept quiet and waited for Chatman to speak first.

"I have some bad news," Chatman began, kneeling down. "Word is out that your mother is dead."

"What did you say?" I asked, not sure I'd heard Chatman correctly.

Bowing his head, he elaborated, "She was killed last night. They say she tried to escape her owner."

"What? What owner? Where did you hear this from?" I was confused and shocked.

"I'm awfully sorry, Sienna," Chatman said.

I shook my head and asked again, "What owner? My mother wasn't in the trade, was she?" I wanted clarification.

Chatman stood up and stroked his goatee.

"Yes," he responded, nodding. "Your mother been in the trade before you were born."

"So she's dead?" I asked, looking up at him.

He turned away and nodded again. "She was killed last night."

"I don't get it," I said. "How do you know this? I mean, were you in touch with her the whole time? Like, did you know her owner or something?"

"No, I haven't been in touch with your mother. But I do know of her owner. This business is pretty small. Everybody in it knows each other," Chatman explained.

"So then you can do something, right?" I asked. "I mean, we can't just let him get away with killing my mom!" The words rolling off my tongue felt surreal.

"It's more to it than that. This business is complicated. You just have to be strong and be grateful that you're here in a safe place."

On that note Chatman turned and walked out of my room.

I didn't know what to make of the news of my mother's sudden death. I was confused, to say the least. I didn't know my mom was in the trade and I felt bad thinking of all she must have gone through. I was filled with questions and, although Chatman was kind of vague, the one thing he was clear about was that I was in a safe place. That fact rang out loud in my mind, making me rethink running away. Then I wondered, was that the purpose of Chatman telling me my mom had been killed? Was that his way of scaring me into staying put?

As I was sitting in my bed, frozen with grief and uncertainty, Ryan appeared in my doorway, a sullen look on his face and in his puffy eyes.

"I'm sorry about your mom," he said, nearing me.

"It's not true, though, is it?" I hoped.

Ryan said nothing.

"Didn't he just say that to keep me from running away?"

Ryan again said nothing, allowing me to ponder the dilemma before me. The tears came unscheduled and it seemed Ryan's arms opened up just in time for me to fall into them. The pain in my heart worsened with every sob. I couldn't tell you how devastated I was. All I knew was that I was in desperate need of love and affection, and I was almost certain I knew where I could get them. It was at that time, on that day, while Chatman and his workers were gone and the other residents were either asleep or a safe distance from my bedroom that I gave up my virginity to Ryan. What started out as him consoling me in his arms turned into the two of us French kissing and from there we were haphazardly guiding each other, him bringing me close and me pulling him in. It was painful, uncomfortable, and all over within minutes. Just like that, we both experienced our first sexual encounter.

"Did I hurt you?" Ryan asked, rolling from on top of me onto his back.

I nodded my head and let out a sigh. "Was it supposed to be like that?" I asked, still teary-eyed.

"I don't know," Ryan said, shrugging his shoulders. He paused, and then confessed, "It felt good to me."

"Somehow, it felt good to me, too," I said. "Just not in a good way," I added.

Ryan kissed me on my lips and then he proceeded to climb over my pain-stiffened body. Midway, he stopped and his mouth dropped, his eyes glued to my midsection.

"What's wrong?!" I nearly screamed, looking down.

My sheets and my pajama shirt were covered in blood. It looked like a crime scene. Immediately, I panicked.

"What did you do?" I asked Ryan, terrified.

"I didn't do anything!" he retorted.

Tears burst through my eyelids and rushed down my cheeks. I was sobbing all over again, feeling more emotional and vulnerable than before.

"What did we do?" I cried.

Ryan jumped to his feet and put on his pants. He grabbed the phone that was on my nightstand and dialed three digits. I presumed he was calling the police. I begged him to hang up, fearing that calling the cops would get us in deeper trouble than what I had already predicted. He ignored my pleas and began explaining to the operator what had just happened.

"Yes, um . . . " he started out. "Me and my girlfriend just um . . . we um . . . we had sex. And um . . . , she's bleeding real badly," he finally completed his sentence.

I didn't know what the operator was asking him, but it was a series of yes or no questions and by the end of the conversation Ryan's worrisome expression relaxed. He hung up the phone and sat down beside me, careful not to sit in the blood. He began to explain to me what the operator had told him about what typically happens when a girl has sex for the first time. Bashfully, I wiped my tears and buried my head in Ryan's chest. He helped me clean up and by the time Chatman had returned home, the two of us were watching *Family Matters,* cracking up at Steve Urkel as if the earlier part of the day never occurred.

Ryan became my boyfriend shortly thereafter. We kept our relationship under wraps, though, because we didn't want the question of us having sex to arise. Although Chatman never came out and said it to me, I knew that he disliked having girls in the house deal with his workers. I remembered him mentioning it the time he had thrown Sophia out. So, I played my part around the house, continuing on as I always had, keeping Ryan around me and still spending a lot of time with him. But it did make things harder. I found myself uncontrollable sometimes in Ryan's presence, like I just wanted to jump on top of him. I couldn't because there would usually be someone around us. But there would be those days when Chatman would leave us alone with A.J. or one of his workers who didn't really supervise us. Those were our times to be together as boyfriend and girlfriend and we took full advantage.

Over time, a void was filled within me and it really made a difference in my life. I began to feel complete, like I was not living in vain, but had a purpose. The emotional connection I shared with Ryan had really brought me happiness. I no longer sought excitement outside of the mansion. All I wanted was right in front of me, sharing everything with me from my thoughts to my hopes down to the air I breathed. I was young but I knew that I loved Ryan, truly, and the greatest feeling was knowing that he loved me the same way.

My sweet sixteen was around the corner and just as the season was changing, so was my attitude. Since my mother's death and the blossoming of my relationship with Ryan, I started to look at life in a whole different light. I realized that I needed to make changes in order to get the most out of what short time we had here on the planet. I had nowhere to run to anymore so leaving Chatman's house wasn't an option. However, I knew that one day I would and when that day came I had to be prepared to stand on my own two feet. I realized that I was no different from the girls Chatman smuggled into the country. The only difference between me and them was that I was already a citizen. Other than that we were all there to do the same thing—be sex slaves. I wasn't all for that notion at first. But after deep thought, I realized that just like the countless girls who had come and gone over the years I had no choice. It would be my only means of providing for myself and eventually getting out on my own. Having no money, no real education, no family, no friends, and no work experience, the trade was all I had and all I knew. So once it was fixed in my head that I would be a worker, I decided to make a plan for myself.

I had noticed that the girls who had come into the house with a plan were usually the ones who made it to the promised land. They were the ones who avoided depression and didn't get caught up with drugs and alcohol. Instead, they would work for ten years, pay off their debts to Chatman, and be free to go, and not empty-handed, either. I'd seen girls make it out of Chatman's house with a few hundred thousand dollars to make new lives for themselves and their families. On the other hand, though, I'd seen more girls get sold off with nothing or be deported back to the country they came from. It was basically the survival of the fittest. And I had made up my mind that I would survive.

To start, I began to open up to many of the girls in the house, wanting to know more about them, about their cultures, their countries, their families, etcetera. I wanted to know what brought them to the United States and how they felt about being there. And I heard it all, from the horror stories of girls who had been repeatedly raped by their owners and other men to the dreams and high hopes of those who were promised money and endless opportunities. There were some girls who were just fourteen and fifteen who were sold by their parents or kidnapped from their villages by police officers, ministers, and other kinds of people they thought they could trust. I took it all in, every story, every goal, every path, and every dream. It was my way of connecting with my mother and her experience in the business and at the same time keeping myself focused on my personal goal of making it out alive.

I also wanted to read between the lines and see where the girls who had failed went wrong and where those who had succeeded went right. I wanted to know the negative and the positive so that I would be able to recognize both. Apparently the trade was a trap, not meant for the women to pay their debts and be free to go. From what I gathered from hearing the girls' stories, the owners made more money off the girls when they failed rather than when they succeeded. That explained why Chatman had gotten rid of both of his top women right before they were able to pay off their debts to him. He made more money selling them at the top of their game than he did collecting the twenty-five thousand or so that they owed him for travel, living, and miscellaneous expenses. Learning the business made me aware of many things. I had to be a top girl, but I also had to be a highly paid, highly desired girl, or else I would be a perfect candidate for selling.

I had to appeal to the wealthiest of Chatman's clients, which would increase my value. I knew that Chatman's main objective was money and if I found a way to make him lots of it then my chances of being sold would be slim to none. Chatman tended to get rid of his top girls, yes, but he was not one to get rid of a cash cow. In order to stick around and be granted my freedom in ten years, I had to be both. So, I trained myself for it.

I read a lot of travel books and magazines to familiarize myself with other places and customs. I had the different girls who Chatman would buy and sell over the years teach me how to speak their languages. With their help and my perseverance, I learned Spanish, French, Italian, and Japanese. I also watched a lot of documentaries and shows about royal families, wealthy businesspeople, and celebrities. Once I learned what things the world's wealthiest people enjoyed, I started reading books and watching shows about those particulars, such as golf, polo, horseback riding, and stocks, bonds, and mutual funds. I was learning everything about the world's elite, where they lived, what they liked, whom they loved, whom they hated, what was important to them—everything. I didn't miss a beat.

Just months away from sixteen at the time, I had my eyes on the prize. I no longer saw myself as a little girl who just wanted to have fun. I was a woman who needed to make a way for herself. I needed direction. Hell, I didn't even know Florida outside Miami Beach. The bottom line was I had one option and one shot to turn that option into an out. For me, the decision was clear. I was going to take it—at all costs.

CHAPTER 5

" **S** pread your legs apart," the photographer said to me. "You have to look inviting."

"Like this?" I asked, creating a gap between my legs.

"Yes, yes," the older white gentlemen said, snapping away with his digital camera. "That's it. Relax. Arch your back a little. Good, good."

I was sitting by the pool in back of Chatman's house. Dressed in lingerie and embellished with makeup, I was having my first photo shoot. Chatman had wasted no time arranging for it, either. My sixteenth birthday was just two days ago. I had a splash party with all the house members and some of Chatman's outside associates and employees. I got a lot of gifts, but the biggest came from Chatman. It was a check for $20,000. I almost choked when I opened the envelope and saw it. My first thought was that I could use the money as a down payment on my own town house. But I should have known that there was a catch. Chatman told me I had to use the money to finance my start in the trade. He handed me a list of things I would need right away, including the clothes, makeup, and props that I would be using for my scheduled photo shoot. I also had to pay the photographer and the Web site designer to add my images and profile to Chatman's already developed Web site. He claimed that he was teaching me how to be independent. I swallowed the bullshit and went ahead shopping.

It was a bright day out and pleasantly warm. I was finishing up my pool scene and getting ready to do some shots inside the house on Chatman's king-size bed. I had been taking pictures since eleven in the morning. It was going on three and I had two more looks to shoot. I was tired, but I have to admit it was kind of fun. I felt like a supermodel in front of the camera. Ryan would peek out every now and again. He made me nervous whenever he did and the photographer would tell him to stop. Don't get me wrong, I wasn't nervous about him seeing me in next to nothing. It was just that I wasn't sure how he was taking the fact that his girlfriend was about to be advertised and offered to other men. We hadn't gotten a chance to discuss it.

"You did well," the photographer told me after shooting the last frame. He shook my hand and told me that he would save the images to a CD and have it for me the next day. From the CD, I would be able to e-mail the photos to the Web designer and he would upload them onto Chatman's site.

I thanked him and paid my tab, then I saw him out. I was on the way to change my clothes and wash my face when I was approached in the hallway by Sammy.

"Yes?" I asked politely, unsure what he could have possibly wanted with me.

He then pulled a sheet of paper from the traveling briefcase in which Ryan stored all the girls' profiles.

"You know, when I took on this job," he began, "it was understood that Chatman and I would have no need to communicate. I knew what I had to do and he knew what he had to do and we each did it, no questions asked. So, when I saw this profile in the briefcase for the second time, I must tell you I was tempted to go to him and see about it."

I looked down at the page with my name, height, weight, and other personal information typed on it. My photograph was attached to it by a paper clip. I was speechless. It had completely slipped my mind that I had staged a profile for myself in the past to get a fake ID. Now that I was to start work, Chatman had given him a new profile. Sammy was suspicious.

Sammy continued, "At first I thought that Chatman just made a mistake and put an old profile in with the new batch. But when I looked at it closely I saw that there were some major differences. I can't see Chatman making such huge errors. I can ask him, but I figure if you can clear it up then that saves me from having to go against our deal of maintaining no communication between us."

I knew where Sammy was going and I did want to save him the trouble of having to mention his suspicions to Chatman. At the same time, I wasn't sure I could trust Sammy. For all I knew he was going to get the truth out of me and still go against his and Chatman's deal and rat me out. It was time for me to use the skills I had learned from being brought up under Chatman's roof. I wasn't his daughter, but I had surely become Chatman's child. I had learned how to be quick on my toes and a master manipulator.

"Ohhh," I said as if a lightbulb had just gone off in my head.

"That first profile was for when Chatman wanted me and Ryan to go down and check out the club he was thinking about buying on Washington Avenue. We needed IDs because you had to be twenty-one to get in. You had to do one for Ryan too, right?"

Sammy's face frowned. "Yeah, I did as a matter of fact," he recalled. Then he quickly changed his demeanor. "Oh, okay, so this one is the actual one that he wants me to use for you starting work?" he asked, holding up the Chatman-made profile.

"Correct," I said.

"Okay. Gotcha," he said, putting the paper back in the briefcase. "I'll have it on schedule."

"All right," I said, walking away from Sammy. "Have a good one," I added just for the hell of it. *Sheesh,* I thought, *that was close.*

The days were winding down and my to-do list was getting shorter. I had gotten the disc with my pictures on it and picked out the few I liked best. I e-mailed them over to the Web designer and he uploaded them onto Chatman's site. My picture was labeled "NEW" and when you clicked on it a page appeared that had more pictures of me alongside my name, age—which was increased by two years—my height, weight, and a list of the languages I spoke. It also had two paragraphs that described my hobbies as playing golf and reading; my life goals, which were to become a financial planner and someday fly a plane; and my personality as an upbeat, outgoing cutie. The page looked nice and it was definitely captivating. I will say that it made *me* want to pay for me.

Once I was on the site, Chatman thought it was time for him to break down the rules of the game. He called me in his office one day and sat me down.

"Usually I have one of my workers do this part. But I wanted to be the one to do it for you." After a brief pause, he went on, "This business is very tricky. There are good guys in it and bad guys in it. My job as your owner is to protect you from the bad guys—however, I'm not going to be with you holding ya hand when you're at these guys' hotel or private residence. So I have to prepare you for the worst, you know what I'm saying? Not to say that you will encounter any of this but it does happen and I have to warn you and show you how to protect yourself in case it comes your way. First, if you're ever in a position where a client is trying to force you to do something and you feel uncomfortable and threatened, you are ordered to do whatever it is he is forcing upon you—"

I didn't expect Chatman to say that and I guess my facial expression showed my shock because Chatman immediately explained himself.

"I know it sounds crazy, but what would you be more willing to give up—minutes of misery or your life?"

"That's a no-brainer," I responded.

Chatman nodded. "Exactly. We can always get the bastard in the morning. But if you're dead and gone, then it doesn't matter whether we get 'im or not, does it? Now, second." Chatman stopped to clear his throat. "If you are ever in a position where a client asks to take you anywhere else besides the place that is told to me at the time he books you, say no unless you are allowed to report the change of place to me. Many girls have disappeared this way. You see, there are some people out there who pose as clients but who are really kidnappers. They know the kind of money that can be made off selling an individual."

"What if they take me by force? I mean . . ." I asked, becoming more and more concerned for my safety.

"Good question. The thing is, these guys who pose as clients but are really kidnappers always stay in hotels. And the way I do things is whenever a client tells me that he'll be spending time with one of mine in a hotel, I get the name of the hotel and send one of my guys by there before I send my girls out. My guy talks to the front desk person and scopes out the place. He finds out what day the client checked in and what day he plans to check out. He brings that information to me and if it seems odd, like for instance, if the client is scheduled to check out that day or the next day, then I don't even bother sending my girl. And even if everything does add up, I still have my guy slide the front desk person a couple of dollars to keep an eye on that room and alert us if anything strange takes place."

"Now, what if I'm at a private residence? Isn't it still a concern for kidnapping?"

"It is, but it's not great. Kidnappers don't kidnap girls from the same state they live in. They usually live in another state, or country for that matter, and they go online looking for girls who are what's called in the business hot commodities. Once they find six or seven in one state, they arrange to hook up with all of them, each on a different day. They fly out to that state, get a hotel room for one or two nights, and kidnap six to seven girls in one week. That's how they do it. So if you get called to meet a guy at his residence you can be sure that he's not a kidnapper."

I started to bite my nails, soaking up all the information Chatman was delivering. I wasn't sure I was ready for the field. But the one thing I knew about Chatman was that he put girls to work at sixteen whether they were ready or not. So I just had to do something that I had sworn I would never ever do—I had to trust him.

There was just one more thing left to be done before I would actually be put on the market. And before that, I had a personal task to complete. I needed to talk things over with Ryan and see where his head was at in all that was going on. One early morning, while the whole house was asleep, I snuck into Ryan's room. I woke him out of his sleep with a passionate kiss on his lips. He opened his eyes and when he saw that it was me he wrapped his arms around me. He squeezed me and kissed me like he had been dying to do so. I didn't complain. With all the preparations for starting work I hadn't been able to spend any time with Ryan. We were both longing to be in each other's arms. Needless to say, we had sex that morning. We briefly discussed my new position and all Ryan had to say about it was, "Don't worry, it won't be for long."

I didn't know what he meant by that and I didn't bother to ask. I was just so happy that he wasn't mad that everything else was neither here nor there. I lay beside him in his bed for a couple of hours. When the sun started to rise, I gave him one last kiss and I tiptoed back into my room and fell asleep.

It was around one o'clock when Chatman woke me, telling me to take a shower and get dressed. He had an appointment for me in a half hour. One of his associates was coming to the house to examine me. His name was Stephen. He was a gynecologist who practiced in Fort Lauderdale. I had met Stephen before in passing when I was younger. He seemed like a nice guy.

When I was drying my hair, I heard the doorbell ring. Figuring it was Stephen, I hurried and pulled my hair back in a bun. Then I went downstairs to greet the doctor.

"Hey, Sienna," Stephen said, smiling.

"Doc, you know where to go," Chatman said. "Come and see me when everything is done." Chatman then turned and went back upstairs.

"Yep," Stephen said to Chatman. "Follow me," he told me.

I walked behind Stephen out of the back of the house, across the side yard, and into the pool house. Stephen had a key and everything. Inside, Stephen led me to a loft area above the main floor. I had never been inside a gynecologist's office before so I couldn't say if it was set up as one, but to me it looked like a dentist's office, with its reclining vinyl lounge chair and an adjustable lamp. Stephen took a clean white paper sheet from a shelf in the loft and laid it out over the chair. He told me he was going to go down to the kitchen to wash his hands and that while he was gone I was to undress from the waist down and cover up with another white paper sheet.

I followed his orders and when he returned upstairs, I was lying on the chair with the sheet covering my private parts. Stephen put on a pair of gloves and then started taking small silver tools out of his doctor bag and placing them in some order on a table beside the chair covered with what looked like Saran Wrap.

"Don't be nervous," he said, tapping my quivering knee. "I'll be extra gentle."

I closed my eyes and clutched my stomach while Stephen gave me a Pap smear. It wasn't as painful as I had thought it would be, but it was very uncomfortable. After Stephen collected whatever samples he needed and sealed everything up, he removed his gloves. I was waiting for him to leave the room so that I could dress. Instead, he turned to me and asked, "Sienna, does Chatman know you're not a virgin?"

"What?" I asked, caught off guard. "Why would you say that?"

Stephen chuckled. "I'm a doctor. I know these things."

I didn't know what to say. All I knew was that I was stuck

once again trying to figure a way out of getting into serious trouble with Chatman.

"You know he'll be very disappointed to find out that you're not. He's invested a lot in you and for him to put you on the market as a virgin is guaranteed money, which is what I know he's aiming for. But he can't do that now with you not being a virgin."

I blurted out, "He doesn't have to know."

"Yes, he does. It's my duty to disclose to him all information regarding the status of his girls. I mean, that's what I get paid to do."

I began to panic. "I'm sure there is a way around this. I mean, he'll kill me if he finds out."

"The only thing I can think of is if . . ." Stephen said, slowly rubbing his hand over my knee.

I jumped up, holding the paper sheet tightly around my bottom half.

"Well, I'll just have to tell 'im," Stephen said, packing up his doctor bag.

"No! Please!" I begged. "I'll do it, okay!" I gave in.

"Thatta girl," Stephen said, walking toward me. "Now lie back down on the chair. This'll only take a minute. We have to get back over to the house before somebody comes over here interrupting us."

I reluctantly lay back down on the chair. He stood up in between my legs, unbuttoned his pants, and pulled his private out. He rubbed it up and down my thigh and I cringed. Next, he was on top of me, penetrating me, and saying all kinds of perverted things out of his mouth.

"Oh, yes, Sienna. You're going to make Chatman a lot of money with this. Um, hum. Chatman will never know about this, okay? Or about anybody else who's been in this cave. Um, and it's still so tight, too. Yeah, it's like a virgin's. I'm sure his clients will never know the difference. Oh, yeah. I remember my wife's used to feel like this. Um. I'm so glad you decided to give it to me. I took this drive up here in the middle of a nice afternoon off, I deserve it. I deserve it. Oh yes. Yes. Yes. Yes. Yes," he panted, ejaculating on my pubic hairs.

As soon as he moved from between my legs, I hopped off the chair and put on my clothes. I didn't care that he was still in the loft. I didn't say anything to him as I let myself out. I just sneered at him and fought tooth and nail to keep a teardrop from falling. Back at the main house, Stephen gave his report to Chatman that it appeared I was a virgin and that he would have my test results back in a week, but not to worry because since I hadn't been sexually active it was nearly impossible for me to have an STD. He told Chatman that he could send me out whenever he wanted, that he didn't have to wait for the test results if he didn't want to. Chatman paid him and sent him on his way with a bottled water that he'd asked for. I felt disgusted. I went into my bathroom and showered again. I buried my clothes in the bottom of my hamper, not wanting to see them ever again. I would have burned them if I wasn't afraid to cause a commotion. I put on some clean clothes and turned on my radio. I lay my head on my pillow and fell asleep to Terry Alexander's show on 99 Jamz.

"It's you I love," I whispered in Ryan's ear as I got ready to leave for my first date.

Ryan nodded and opened the door for me. I stepped outside and got into the black tinted-out limousine that was waiting in the driveway. I gave the driver the address to my client's Ocean Drive condominium in Hollywood, Florida. I sipped champagne during the drive and tried to calm my nerves. My mind was racing with thoughts of all the things Chatman told me to do in case I sensed trouble. I wondered what my client would look like. Would he be old or young? Would he smell good? Would he be a gentleman or a jerk? I was uneasy.

We arrived at the beachfront sixteen-story building. The driver assisted me out of the limo and I walked into the lobby. Before I could approach the front desk, a tall, thin, orange-skinned, bleached-hair, porcelain-veneer-wearing guy walked up to me.

"Sienna?" he asked, revealing his too-perfect pearly whites.

"Yes." I smiled back, but only half as wide.

"I'm Harold," he said. "Right this way."

Harold and I rode the elevator to the twelfth floor. Harold's unit was a short walk down the hall. The inside of his two-bedroom, two-bathroom home was stark white, like his teeth, from the kitchen cabinets to the floors and even the furniture.

"Welcome to my place," Harold said. "Get comfortable, make yourself at home. Can I get you anything to drink?"

I started to request juice, but changed my mind at the thought of him slipping a date-rape drug inside it.

"No, thank you."

"Well, have a seat," he said.

"This is a beautiful view," I told him, happy to have found one good thing to comment on.

Through the glass sliding doors in his living room I could see boats passing by on the deep blue sea.

"So, I read online that you speak Italian," Harold said to me while pouring himself a glass of red wine.

"Si," I answered. *"Esatto."*

"Sei bella," Harold told me, sipping his wine.

"Grazie."

Harold smiled grandly as he drank his wine. He played some music and asked me to dance with him. He led me in a waltz and was pretty impressed with my knowledge of ball-room dancing. At that time I started to loosen up. Harold was not my type, but he was indeed fun. Sure, it felt like I was dancing with my grandpa, but as long as it was just dancing I wasn't complaining. The sun began to set over the ocean. The sky dimmed. Harold and I ordered Italian and had it delivered to us. We ate, talked, and watched back-to-back episodes of *Family Feud*. At eight o'clock Harold got a call from the lobby that my driver was waiting. Harold ended our date with an old-fashioned kiss on my hand and then he saw me on the elevator. As the doors closed, he flashed his cosmetically intact fronts one last time.

"Ciao," I said, waving good-bye.

I got inside the limo, leaned my head against the headrest, and dozed off.

My first date was over and it went nothing like I had expected, but exactly how I would have hoped. I didn't have to do anything sexual with Harold, which would have grossed me out, and at Chatman's $800 per hour rate, I banked $2,400. If only all my dates would end up that way.

CHAPTER 6

"Chatman, please," Brighton, an obnoxious Fort Lauderdale attorney, demanded through the phone.

I was putting my clothes back on as the perturbed Brighton waited for Chatman to take his call. I was worried, scared to go home. I had no idea how Chatman would react to what Brighton was about to tell him.

"Chatman, it's me, Brighton. Listen, I put in a request for a virgin and surely that's not what I've gotten. Now, I don't know if you're trying to play games with me or not, but . . ."

Chatman must have been speaking as Brighton's complaints came to a pause. I strained my eardrums trying to make out the chatter coming from Brighton's headset.

"What do you mean, you assure me? You can't piss on my head and tell me it's raining. I've been with virgins before and this girl isn't one. Now, fill my request or refund me my sixteen hundred!" Another pause, then Brighton continued, "She's putting her clothes back on. There's nothing I want with her at all!

"Yes, I know I spent an hour with her already, but had I known up front that she wasn't what I had asked for, then trust me when I tell you, I would have sent her back immediately." Brighton grew red and he started to rub his forehead in frustration. "You know, it is very unprofessional how you're handling this. I wouldn't expect for you to conduct business this way. I'm leaving her out front and I want my money back. That's that!" Brighton snapped, snatching his phone's headset off. He turned to me and said, "As soon as you're done dressing, there's the door."

Sitting out in front of the newly opened Loews Hotel watching all the guests go in and out, I had never felt so low in my life. Of all times, I got put out during the hotel's grand opening week. There were herds of people passing me by, looking at me with turned-up noses. I wasn't sure if it was my exotic looks or my rather revealing outfit that made the ladies rush their mates past me. But they all seemed overprotective of the men on their arms, some looking like they wanted to go as far as covering their man's eyes. Little did they know, I didn't want their men and the way I was feeling, I doubted their men wanted me. According to Brighton, I was used up and worthless. No man of such status would ever want me. So it was absolutely nothing for the passersby to be concerned about. I wanted to cry but I didn't want to make a scene. Instead, I sat there, pitiful, waiting for my ride and my punishment.

"Sienna!" Chatman called out the moment I stepped foot in the house. *"Come up here!"*

Dreading the walk up the stairs to Chatman's office, my body was quivering. I'd never been beaten by Chatman before, but I've seen it done and I was almost certain that that would be my fate for having deceived him about being a virgin. In this business, according to Chatman, a virgin was his most precious asset. Then to top it off, I made him look like a fool in front of one of his clients and possibly caused him to lose that client.

Chatman's eyebrows were bent and his eyes could have cut me in half. He was sitting at his desk with his hands folded under his chin.

"Tell me what's going on," he commanded, calmly but stern.

I didn't want to confess, but Chatman already knew the truth so lying would just add fuel to the fire.

"I'm not a virgin," I murmured.

"No shit!" Chatman's loud raspy voice bounced off the walls. "Who?" he asked, back in his calm and stern tone.

The tears got in formation and began to march out of my eyes. I shook my head from left to right and I cried out, "I can't tell."

Chatman leaped from his seat and grabbed me by my arms. "I'm not one for games, Sienna, and you of all people know this! Now, you're willing to defend this guy, that's fine, but it's your ass that'll be left in the fire. Which do you choose?"

Unable to look in Chatman's eyes, I bowed my head and responded, "I can't."

Chatman angrily pulled me out of his office and down the steps, practically dragging me. Through my water-filled eyes I noticed Ryan looking over the banister, watching us.

"You wanna be a whore? I'll treat you like a whore!" Chatman shouted for the whole house to hear. "You cost me money and a good working relationship with one of my best clients pulling a stunt like this!! You saw that I marketed you as a virgin! And you said nothing! Do you know what I could do to you?"

Chatman pulled me out the back door and took me to one of the detached garages. He threw me inside and told me that I wouldn't eat or drink until I told him who I'd lost my virginity to. Then he sent the ultimate threat: "And I dare it to be one of my guys! I swear on my life, I will sell you right back to the man who killed your dad! And I won't think twice!!"

The garage door slowly closed and Chatman was out of sight. I dropped to the concrete floor and lowered my head to my knees. I cried for hours it felt like, until I fell asleep. When I awoke, I cried some more. Painful memories of my father's murder flooded my mind and the horrible feelings of isolation and intense fear reminded me of the days I had spent alone in the shack, hungry and thirsty, clinging to life. I panicked. I ran to the garage door and started banging on it, screaming for somebody to help me. After a while, I was too tired to continue and I sat in a corner and cried some more. It was dark and getting cold. I guessed nightfall was approaching. I didn't know how long Chatman had planned for me to stay locked up in the garage, but if it was dependent upon me coming clean about Ryan, then I would probably die there. There was no way I was telling him the truth after he'd said he would sell me back to the one man whom I sincerely hated.

Panic overcame me again as I started to feel hunger pangs coming on. I tried my luck at the door once more, banging and screaming, screaming and banging. I hoped that maybe A.J. or someone would be pulling into one of the other garages and hear my pleas. If only I could get a breath of fresh air, it was worth it to me. Anything to relieve the claustrophobia I was experiencing. But nothing transpired besides me losing my energy and falling to the ground again in tears. I repeated the hopeless process throughout the night, guessing that Ryan was just waiting for Chatman to go to bed before he came out and rescued me. I was wrong. No one came. No one answered. I spent that night and the next three alone in the garage, hungry, parched, weary, and afraid. I became so desperate at times that I would lick the walls of the garage just for a taste of something.

One morning or afternoon—it was hard for me to tell the difference—I heard the garage door opening. I lifted my head, which seemed like it weighed a ton, to see who it was. Although it didn't show, I felt a boost of energy when I saw Ryan. He walked over to me and picked me up off the floor. Carrying me out of the garage, he apologized to me repeatedly.

"Did you tell her?" Chatman asked as we entered the kitchen.

Still apparently upset, he was leaning against the counter with his arms folded across his chest. "This man must love you," he started out. "The minute he found out that your ass was starving to death in that garage, he 'fessed up to me—even after I made an announcement that I was putting whoever you messed around with out of this house. What do you have to say to that?" Chatman had a smirk on his face and he looked at me with an evil eye.

I quickly recalled his threat that if he found out I had messed with one of his guys he would sell me to my father's killer. Weak and somewhat incoherent, I still managed to come up with a plan.

"Why did you lie?" I asked Ryan, who had sat me down on a bar stool. "Why did you take the blame?"

Ryan didn't say anything. He appeared confused. Chatman, on the other hand, inquired, "Oh, you're ready to talk now?"

"Chatman, I never slept with Ryan," I said. "He probably just said that to end my suffering. He does love me. He's my best friend."

Chatman grew agitated. "Then who was it if it wasn't Ryan?"

"It was Stephen," I said, tears sliding down my face.

"Stephen? You expect me to believe that?"

"Think about it. If I wasn't a virgin don't you think he would have been able to see that when he examined me? And wouldn't he have told you?"

I had everybody's undivided attention.

"He raped me that day in the pool house and that's how I lost my virginity. He told me that if I told you he would deny it and say that it was me who tried something with him and he said that he knew for a fact that you would get rid of me because you didn't tolerate your girls doing things with your workers. He said that as long as you never found out we would both be okay and he assured me that none of your clients would be able to tell that I wasn't a virgin after having sex only once."

"Are you playing games with me?" Chatman asked.

Looking Chatman straight in his eyes, I shook my head. "No," I said.

"I'll get to the bottom of this," Chatman said, leaving the kitchen. "And when I do, somebody is going to pay."

I was in my bathroom spitting up the McDonald's I had just finished. I think I had eaten it too fast and it made me sick to my stomach. There was a pounding on my door.

"Here I come," I said, wiping my mouth with a tissue.

I opened the bathroom door and Chatman and some other man I had never seen before were standing in my room.

"Sienna, did Stephen use a condom?' Chatman asked straightforwardly.

I shook my head no.

"Where are the panties you were wearing?" he followed up with another blunt question.

I took a moment to think about it, and then I walked over to my hamper. I dug the clothes out and reached the outfit I had on the day I was examined. I picked up a pair of purple panties and held them out to Chatman. The unfamiliar man reached out and grabbed them using something that looked like a pair of prongs. He placed them in a Ziploc bag.

Without saying anything, Chatman and the man left my room. Shortly after, Ryan came in.

"You all right?" he asked me.

"Yeah," I said, sitting on my bed.

"What was that about?" he asked, sitting beside me.

"I guess they wanna see if I'm telling the truth or not."

Ryan shook his head. "You shouldn't have done that," he said. "You're digging a deeper hole."

"No I'm not. I saved us both."

"How? When Chatman finds out that you lied you're just going to get in more trouble and I'll still be kicked out."

"But I'm not totally lying. Ryan, Stephen did rape me that day."

The look on Ryan's face was unforgettable. "What?"

"I didn't want to tell you."

"Sienna, what do you mean you didn't want to tell me? We tell each other everything. When did that change?"

"I didn't want you to look at me differently."

"Are you serious? I wouldn't look at you differently for something like that! You should have told me. I would have fuckin' hurt that pussy!" Ryan said, rubbing the peach fuzz on his chin.

"I'm sorry," I said, covering my face with my palms.

Ryan put his arms around me and said, "Don't be. It wasn't

your fault. And when Chatman finds out that what you said did happen, Stephen'll get what's his. I just hope I'm the one he orders to give it to 'im."

Ryan's wish came true. A DNA test proved that Stephen did have sex with me. As far as him being the one whom I lost my virginity to, that couldn't be argued. Chatman didn't want to hear anything Stephen had to say once it was determined that his semen was in my panties. He felt betrayed by Stephen and that was the one thing Chatman didn't tolerate. He was in a business where trust and loyalty were crucial. They were two qualities that his livelihood depended on. If he found out that for one second either of the two had been forsaken he was bound to unleash a wrath that no one could stand.

And that is exactly what occurred. Stephen was in Chatman's office begging for Chatman's forgiveness. Then Ryan was instructed to drive him home. On his way out the door, Stephen was thanking Chatman profusely for sparing his life. The next thing we knew, a funeral invitation had been delivered to Chatman by Stephen's widow. Though it was never confirmed or denied that Ryan was the one who had carried out Stephen's murder, it was heavily speculated, and weeks after the funeral, which Chatman not only attended but paid for, Ryan was granted a promotion.

Slowly but surely things got back on track at the house. I had been requested by several of Chatman's clients and money continued to pour in on my behalf. Chatman was even able to rebuild his relationship with Brighton after he explained the story to him. I had gotten over the whole episode and worked toward moving on. In the process, I realized that I had a lot of emotional issues that I needed to deal with. I was very insecure and unhappy, though I almost always kept a smile on my face. Inside, however, I was burning. I started reading spiritual books, trying to fill the void. They helped me from day to day, but in life there is always something and just as I was growing past the pain, more issues came my way.

One day I woke up late, around two in the afternoon. I had stayed up the night before reading a good book. I washed my face and brushed my teeth, then I headed downstairs to get something to eat. I noticed it was very quiet in the house, and figured Chatman had gone out and all the girls were either on dates or in their rooms. I had no idea where Ryan was and guessed he was out with Chatman or on his own taking care of business. He had become busier since receiving his most recent promotion. In fact, I hardly saw him anymore. It seemed that whenever I was home he was out, and whenever he was home I was out. And the days that we were both home at the same time, I kind of distanced myself from him. He didn't like it, I could tell, but it was for our own good. What Chatman had told me he would do if I ever messed with one of his workers stuck in the back of my mind. It made me a lot more cautious and even though I desperately wanted to be with Ryan, I knew that I would be skating on thin ice if I did. Ryan didn't quite understand. I never did tell him about the threat that Chatman made.

Anyhow, I started to go down the steps when I heard noises. I looked around at all the closed doors and tried to locate the sounds. I backed away from the stairs and walked down the hall, putting my ear to all the doors. Finally I got to Ryan's door and pinpointed where the noise was coming from. I slowly turned the knob and opened his door.

Ryan and one of the girls who lived in the house were in the bed, naked, having sex. The two of them stopped and looked up at me in shock. I think they were relieved that I wasn't Chatman, but still embarrassed that they had been caught. Ryan gently tossed the girl off of him and sat up in his bed. He was looking at me with so much regret in his eyes. But it was too late for that. I lost control and ran over to him and started whaling on him. The girl tried to intervene and after she realized she was no help, she put on her clothes and scurried out of Ryan's room.

I don't know all of what I was saying and doing to him outside of calling him every name in the book and striking him with my balled fists. But he was catching a whole lot of backlash. Every angry and hurt moment that I had experienced up to that point was being taken out on Ryan. I had been giving him work for at least five minutes and that's a long time for a fight. And I guess he felt like he deserved it because he showed little resistance. He only tried to run away from me rather than hitting me back, which would have stopped me eventually. I ran after him, chasing him around every square foot of his room, hitting him every chance I got. It wasn't until I got tired that he was able to get relief. At that point I burst into tears, finally allowing what I had walked in on to sink in.

"Why, Ryan?!" I asked, breathless.

Ryan didn't say anything. He just stood in the corner staring at me sorrowfully.

"What? Are you with her now or something? I mean, all you had to do was tell me. Just say, 'Sienna, it's not working out. I wanna be with somebody else.' Why did you have to go behind my back? And then to do it right in here, knowing I was still in the house."

Ryan finally spoke up. "I didn't know you were in the house."

I looked at him, disgusted. "Oh, so, it was cool as long as I wasn't in the house?"

"No, no, I didn't mean it like that. I'm just saying that I would never disrespect you like that," Ryan protested.

"Disrespect me? Ryan, however you look at it, you've disrespected me!"

"I know and I'm sorry! I swear to God, I'm sorry!"

"Why, though?" I asked. "I don't understand. What did I do to you?"

Ryan wiped his face with his palm. "Sienna, it's been hard on me lately, you working and all—"

I cut him off. "You said it wouldn't affect anything! You know I don't have a choice so don't even try to put this on me working!"

"I know that!" Ryan whined. "But just hear me out, please!"

I sat on the edge of Ryan's bed. My leg began to tremble. "Go 'head. I wanna hear this!"

"First of all, let me just say that I am not excusing what I did in any way. And I know that I'm one hundred percent wrong for cheating on you. But you working ain't been sittin' well with me—"

"But—!"

"Let me finish, Sienna, please!"

Taking heavy breaths, I said, "Go 'head."

"I know that I said it wouldn't bother me, and it hasn't. But lately you've been distant from me, like you don't want to be with me anymore, and I can't help but think that maybe you've grown some feelings for your clients that you might not be able to control. I'm feeling like I'm the second man. Like maybe you've moved on. I mean, we don't get to spend time with each other like that anymore so I would think that the one chance we do get to be together you would jump at it. But no, you'd rather read your books. You can read anytime! You can read when Chatman is here. You can't be with me when Chatman is here. I just don't get it," Ryan explained.

I didn't have much of a comeback, because what Ryan said was true. While I called myself protecting us, I hadn't been considerate of his feelings. However, he should have come to me and talked to me about how he was feeling instead of going to somebody else. There was no excuse for what he had done. He not only cheated on me, but he did it with somebody I have to look at every day, and right there in his bed. He crossed the line.

"Well, Ryan, for your information, when Chatman found out that I wasn't a virgin, he told me that if he found out that I had been with one of his guys he would sell me back to the man who killed my father. And maybe I should have told you this before, but the reason I was distant from you was because I was scared to death about being caught. I knew that if Chatman so much as suspected I was dealing with you he would go through with his threat. And I'm sorry, but I refuse to let that happen. I will get on my knees and beg for God to take my life before I put myself in that position. So, I'm sorry if I haven't been spending that kind of time with you or if I've been trying to avoid that kind of contact with you, but I had my reasons and I feel like they are beyond justified." I wiped my face and stood up. I looked at Ryan and shook my head in disbelief. I wanted to say more, but I felt it was no use. There was no sense crying over spilled milk. I had said what I had to say. I left his room and went to my own. God knows I no longer had an appetite.

Ryan came to my room a few times trying to get me to let him in, but I ignored him. I just picked up my spiritual books and forced myself to read. And although the books encouraged turning the other cheek, I couldn't get my mind off plotting revenge. Without even trying, I came up with a plan.

Days after I had caught Ryan cheating on me I politely knocked on Chatman's office door. He told me to come in and I told him I needed to talk to him about something important.

"What is it?" Chatman asked.

"One of the girls in this house is trouble," I said.

Chatman sat back in his chair and shrugged his shoulders. "What do you mean?"

"Sandy tried to come on to Ryan and when he denied her she wouldn't give up. She actually told him she didn't care what your rule was, she was determined to be with him."

"If this is so, why wouldn't Ryan have come and told me? He's the one who owes me the loyalty to do so."

"Ryan is a nice guy but he's on the naïve side, we both know that," I said. "I don't think he wanted to get anybody in trouble. And the only reason I'm telling you this is because I overheard Sandy telling another girl that she wasn't here to be nobody's slave. She said she was here to take over your business and that she was going to use Ryan to do it. She said that Ryan was the only one not smart enough to see through her and that he would be the easiest to target because he was still wet behind the ears."

"Oh, yeah?" Chatman asked, seemingly analyzing my story in his head.

I nodded. "She's plotting a major scheme against you. And you don't need a seed like that planted in your house."

Chatman nodded. "That's for sure," he said, then coughed softly. "I appreciate you coming and telling me this. I'll see what's going on and I'll handle it. You just keep this conversation between us for now, okay?"

"Okay," I agreed and turned to walk out his office.

"Sienna," Chatman called out.

I stopped and turned around.

"You don't have any reasons to lie to me, do you?"

"No," I said, straight up.

"Well, go get Sandy, Ryan, and the girl who you heard Sandy telling her plot to and bring them all here. I think we should get to the bottom of this right now."

"Okay," I said, not flinching at all. Chatman was testing me and if I had stalled or started changing my story he would have known that I was full of shit and my plan would have back-fired.

I walked down the hall and knocked on Ryan's door first. While I waited for him to open it, I was conjuring up a plan B. I must admit, though, I was sweating a little bit.

"Ryan, Chatman wants you in his office," I said, without making eye contact with him.

As I was making my way to the room that Sandy stayed in, I heard Chatman call me.

"Yes?" I asked, standing halfway in his office and halfway in the hall.

"Don't get Sandy just yet."

Just then Ryan stiffened up. I knew he was probably ready to shit in his pants. He shot me a pitiful look and scratched his head like he was trying to come up with a defense. I laughed inside at the fear he displayed. *Yeah, go 'head and sweat. That's what ya ass get,* I thought.

"Ryan, Sienna just let me in on something that occurred between you and Sandy."

Oooh, I wish I had a camera to capture the paranoia on this nigga's face!

"Chatman," Ryan began.

"No, don't explain. Just keep your distance from her from here on out. Understood?" Chatman kept it short and simple.

"Done!" Ryan said with enthusiasm.

"All right, you can leave," Chatman told him.

But just like an ass kisser he had to say something to try to make up for what he did. "Chatman, I'm sorry. I shouldn't have let it go there." He sounded sincere, giving me a look as if those words were meant for me, too.

Nigga, please, I thought. *Just be happy I ain't fry ya ass like I wanted to.*

"Sienna, can you tell Sandy I want to see her? And who was the other girl?"

This was the part I regretted. I didn't want to get any innocent people in trouble but I had no choice. It was either me or her, whomever I decided *she* would be. "Sonia," I lied.

"Tell both of them to come here and then you can go about your business."

I did what I was told. Sandy and Sonia walked past me toward Chatman's office with perplexed looks on their faces. Well, let me rephrase that. Sonia was perplexed, but Sandy looked upset, like she knew I'd ratted her out. And that was the last time I saw either of them. From what I was told, Chatman sent them both on dates that very night and never had anybody pick them up.

From that day on, things changed within me. I started walking around Chatman's house with my head to the ceiling. I felt like a boss and I dared anybody to cross me. A tough aura surrounded me, like a barrier protecting me from harm. My new "self-preservation" attitude not only helped me in the house, but it prepared me for the world.

CHAPTER 7

*T*urning eighteen meant I was able to start doing what I wanted . . . well, to a certain extent. Let's just say Chatman gave me more leeway. He okayed my dying my hair honey blonde and he even allowed me to get breast implants.

I had just awakened from my surgery and I was in so much pain. My surgeon gave me some medication that was supposed to ease my discomfort, but I was still waiting for it to kick in. I could feel the difference in my breasts. I had gone from a 32B to a 32D and I could tell they were much fuller and firmer. I was excited about having it done and couldn't wait to be able to show them off. Big breasts were definitely an asset in my line of work. Chatman knew that and I think that was the only reason he gave me the green light.

I was accompanied by Ryan, whom Chatman had grown to trust more. He was justified, too, because Ryan hadn't touched another one of his girls since Chatman told him to stay away from Sandy almost two years ago. He didn't even pursue the fling we once had. We both felt we were better off friends. Our jobs wouldn't allow for anything more. Ryan was in the waiting room for the ninety minutes it took to have the surgery done. Then he was able to come back to my room.

"How do you feel?" he asked, walking toward me slowly.

Somewhat dazed, I responded, "Sore."

"Yeah, well, the doctor said that you would have some swelling for at least a week."

"I know. Maybe two weeks. But he said this bra would help," I said, lifting my gown and showing Ryan the surgical bra the doctor had me wearing.

"Daaammmnnnn," Ryan said, sounding like Craig and Smokey in *Friday*. "Them things is huge!"

I cracked a half smile and chuckled. "You are so stupid."

"Chatman sent the wrong one for this. Shit, I'm catchin' feelings again," Ryan joked.

"Too bad. These are all mine," I joked back.

Ryan and I joked back and forth for a little while until the doctor came in. He gave me final instructions for how to shower, how to sleep, how to raise my arms, etcetera, then he helped me change into my shirt. He made Ryan watch everything closely and told him that he needed to stay with me for at least twenty-four hours. Ryan complied and he assisted me out of the office. Bent over, scarred, and bruised, I left the South Florida Center for Cosmetic Surgery a new woman.

When Ryan and I got home, he took me straight to my room. He made me a bowl of clam chowder soup and poured me a glass of water. He served me in bed and catered to me for the rest of that day into the night and throughout that next day. He was a real help, reminding me of what I could and couldn't do and putting himself at my beck and call. I was grateful for him taking time out of his schedule to be my nurse. God knows Chatman wouldn't have done it and the girls kept such late hours, they were mostly asleep during the day.

I felt better with each passing day. The swelling decreased and I began to resume my normal activities, like laundry and making my own food. Ryan got back to his day-to-day routine but still checked in on me in his spare time. For the most part, though, he was in and out, working hard to prove himself in every way to Chatman in hopes of being his right hand on the new shipment Chatman was planning. I believed he would as he had really matured over the years and had begun to be recognized as a stand-up guy. Chatman hardly said as much, but it was obvious he was impressed with Ryan's leadership and initiative. He constantly gave Ryan more duties and let him in on more business meetings. Ryan was learning the game inside and out and he was becoming an asset to Chatman's team. I was proud of him, but still slightly jealous. Ever since he came to live with us, I sensed competition. Maybe it was just me. However, I was making strides in my own path, and I could tell that Chatman was impressed with my achievements as well. So it was more healthy competition than anything.

The moment that my new pictures were posted on Chatman's Web site, the requests came pouring in. Men from all over were offering to empty their wallets for a date with me, particularly for the Fourth of July. Chatman used the high demand to his advantage and increased my hourly rate. He wanted to weed out the phonies from the real power players. Sure enough, some of the men backed down, but there was still quite a significant number asking for me. So Chatman decided to up the ante and had the Web designer post an online auction for me. It was the first time Chatman had done something like that. The bids started at $850 an hour for five hours minimum and quickly rose to $1,200 an hour for ten hours minimum, and they kept coming the whole day. Chatman was about to accept one of the best offers when a bid came in that knocked all the rest out of the water. A European trader offered $2,800 a day for thirty days minimum. That totaled $84,000. Chatman told me to pack my bags.

I didn't know what I was in for, but I felt confident that I would have a good time. Chatman ran thorough background checks on the client I was meeting in Rome. He found out that the client was well known and well respected in Italy and that in addition to being a trader he was a very prosperous land developer. He owned several hotels throughout the world. He had recently gone through a nasty divorce with his third wife and needed a vacation badly. He saw my picture and thought I would be the perfect person to spend it with and when he saw the bids he was really determined to have me.

After over thirteen hours of traveling, including a two-hour layover in Paris-De Gaulle, I arrived at the Leonardo da Vinci (Fiumicino) Airport on Tuesday, July 3. Transportation picked me up and drove me to the Westin Excelsior in Rome's Via Veneto district. I was escorted to the Villa Cupola, supposedly the largest suite in all of Europe. When I entered the suite, I thought I had walked into paradise. I had never seen anything so astonishing in my life. The suite was so big, I almost forgot I was in a hotel. I was told it took up two full floors. Everything, from the furnishings to the original artwork, down to the floral arrangements on the terrace, was grand. Regal drapes covered the massive windows. The living room's dome-shaped ceiling soared up at least forty feet and was covered in frescoes, which were paintings made by brushing watercolors onto fresh damp plaster. It reminded me of the ceilings in the Venetian Hotel in Vegas I had seen on the Travel Channel.

Laid out with a paneled dining room, a private fitness room, a theater, a sauna, a steam bath, and a Jacuzzi, the suite was close to the size of Chatman's mansion in Miami. I was in awe. I scrambled to remember all the things I had learned about the wealthy. Surely it would come into play during the next four weeks. I had stepped into a whole different realm of luxury. How was I possibly going to fit in? I didn't even want to unpack, feeling that my clothes were too meager to be worn in such a place. Suddenly, I felt inadequate. I wanted to go back to the airport and fly back to my comfort zone. Why did this man have to choose me? I questioned myself.

"Sienna." A man's voice startled me.

I turned around and behind me was a short, dark-skinned, dark-haired white guy dressed in tan linen pants and a navy short-sleeved polo shirt. He had a pair of flip-flops on his feet. He was quite attractive and youthful looking, contrary to what I expected from a rich divorcé in his late fifties.

"Yes. And you are?" I asked, holding out my hand for an introductory shake.

"I'm Andrew," he said with a smirk as if I should have known. Then he moved my hand out of the way and leaned in, kissing me once on each cheek.

"Oh, of course," I said, returning the kisses. How could I have forgotten the most important thing? Everybody knew how Italians greeted one another.

"I'm glad you made it here safely," he said, handing me a glass of red wine. "Please sit down."

I sank into the cozy fabric of the antique-meets-modern

sofa. I put my pocketbook beside me and sipped the wine slowly.

"Before we begin this monthlong vacation together, I thought it might be best if we spend the first day or two getting to know each other a bit. What do you think?"

"That's a good idea," I said, slightly swirling my glass.

"I know you're probably exhausted from the flight, so we can give each other a quick rundown and then I'll leave you to yourself. How does that sound?"

I nodded my head in agreement. "Sounds good."

"Well," he said, repositioning himself on the couch. "My name is Andrew, as I said. I was born and raised in the United States. I got married after earning my master's degree in business. My first wife and I divorced after seven years. She wanted to have kids really badly and I was too hung up on jump-starting my career so we eventually had to call it splits. I married again at thirty-five, which was stupid because I hardly knew the woman. We had only dated six and a half months before I proposed to her on a whim. We lasted two years. In the meantime, my career was really blossoming and that was what I focused on. I visited Europe often to meet with clients whose money I invested for them and on one visit I came across a really great investment opportunity. I wound up getting into land development and decided to move here for good. This is where I met my third ex-wife." Andrew's eyebrows raised. "We tied the knot on my forty-fifth birthday and made it work for eleven years. Who said the third's the charm? What do they know?" Andrew joked.

"Well, I'm sorry I don't have any failed marriages to brag about, but I can give you a little history," I said, feeling a buzz from the wine.

Andrew chuckled. "I like you already," he said.

"My name is Sienna. I'm an only child. I grew up in Miami mostly, on Star Island, so I'm what Americans call a socialite. I like going out and enjoying myself."

"So you know some pretty famous people, then, huh?"

I nodded. "I know their children, yeah, but not necessarily them, you know what I mean?"

"Totally," Andrew said, gazing into my eyes. "You're very beautiful."

"Thank you," I told him, trying not to blush.

"Well, I think I'll keep my word and give you some alone time," he said, snapping out of his dreamy state.

Andrew took my empty wineglass and set it on the table. "The butler will get this." Then he walked me to the master bedroom. "Get comfortable. Use the Jacuzzi or you can call for a massage or something. Whatever you want. Don't be shy. I'm going to meet with one of my partners for dinner. I'll be back around eight, nine at the latest, all right?"

"All right, I'll see you when you get back."

Andrew kissed me good-bye and headed out of the suite, leaving me alone.

At first I just sat on the bed trying to think of things to do. Then I decided to tour the suite. When I got back to the master bedroom, I was in the mood for a nice cold rainfall shower. Afterward, I started to put on my pajamas, but the plush complimentary bathrobe was so comfortable, I didn't want to take it off. I oiled my body with my favorite strawberry and cinnamon buttermilk moisturizing lotion. I grabbed the July issue of *Vogue* magazine that I had already read from front to back during my trip and I went out and sat on the terrace to enjoy the nice night air. I munched on some grapes and crackers and I helped myself to another glass of wine. I felt brushed off at first, but eventually I was happy that Andrew had left me all alone. I needed that time of peace and tranquillity.

My monthlong stay with Andrew ended up being more adventurous than I thought I could handle. For the first two weeks we patronized the hotel, dining at their restaurants and ordering their spa services. We had sex on occasion, but Andrew seemed to be delighted at just being in my company. The next two weeks were when the games began. Andrew took me to a Hawaiian-themed birthday party for a friend of his. There were plenty of model-type women there dressed in hula skirts and bikini tops, but for some reason the eyes of all the men seemed to be glued to me. Andrew whispered in my ear that it was because I was so exotic-looking. He told me that European men loved an exotic-looking woman. I didn't feel uncomfortable about it; it was an extreme confidence booster. But what took me by surprise was when Andrew offered me to one of them. I didn't know whether to go with it or not. Chatman hadn't warned me of such a situation.

I danced with the guy almost the entire party and when it was time to go back to the hotel, Andrew asked if I wanted to stay there at the guy's house with him. I pulled him to the side and expressed to him that I would rather go back with him. Then he laughed and thanked me for being polite. He told me that he knew that I liked the guy and that the guy liked me. His exact words were "You might as well make five thousand dollars screwing someone you like."

"What do you mean?" I asked.

"Do you know why I paid seventy-five thousand dollars to spend thirty days with you?"

I remained silent.

"Because I knew that I could make seventy-five thousand dollars off you in just fifteen days. So you see, I really got my two weeks in for free," he explained with a smile. "Now, you do have a choice in this. I mean, I wouldn't force a woman to do anything. I don't have to. It's completely up to you. But if you do this, then I'll return the favor and give you ten thousand for yourself."

"When you say ten thousand for myself, what do you mean exactly?"

"I mean without involving Chatman. He doesn't have to know."

I thought about it and asked, "He's going to be suspicious when I bring ten thousand dollars in his house. I mean, where would I keep it, in my sock drawer?" I was being sarcastic.

Andrew frowned and said, "Oh, don't worry about that. I have a place you can put it." Then he added, "You are new to this business, I know, but if you plan to go far you have to start thinking like an owner instead of like a slave. I know plenty of contractors who work for a company but who do things on the side." Andrew winked. "You know what I mean."

I nodded my head. "I'll follow your lead," I said.

That night I stayed with Andrew's friend, Colin, in his luxury apartment on Piazza Navona. We had sex and he handed me a check for $5,000. He gave me an additional thousand in cash. The night after, I stayed at the International Palace in Via Nazionale, the heart of the Eternal City, with a banker named Thomas. Another check was written and five hundred in cash exchanged hands. The next night I spent with Sam at the Hotel Morgana, which was walking distance from the Coliseum. Then it was Raul at his home in Prati district, and Edward at his apartment on the Piazza Farnese. Then I was with Anthony at the St. Regis Grand, and the list goes on.

When it was all said and done I had visited just about every high-end neighborhood, square, historic building, and hotel that Rome had to offer. I had seen many monuments like the Sistine Chapel and the Trevi Fountain. I had been wined and dined by some of the finest, most wealthy European men. And on top of it all I had made $10,000 from Andrew and collected an additional $9,000 in tips.

On my last day in Europe, Andrew and I flew to Zurich so that Andrew could show me where to keep my money as he had promised. He took me to a Swiss bank and, after he explained how to open a numbered account, he walked me over to his friend, a young, good-looking Japanese guy, who happened to be the senior bank officer.

"*Ohayou gozaimasu,*" I said, lowering my head.

Apparently impressed, the guy smiled and paused, seemingly speechless. Andrew ended the awkward silence between us and introduced his friend.

"Sienna, this is Tomio. Tomio, Sienna."

"*Hajimemashite,*" Tomio said, deciding to test my Japanese beyond good morning.

"*Genki desu. Anata wa?*" I responded.

"*Watashi mo genki desu,*" he said, then he added, "*Arigatou.*"

"*Arigatou gozaimasu,*" I said, lowering my head once more.

Tomio turned to Andrew and said, "Beauty and skill? They're not usually coupled."

"She's one of a kind," Andrew said.

I smiled and then we all refocused on the business at hand. Tomio explained the security and legal aspects of Swiss banking and broke everything down to me in simplest terms. I handed him over my ten-thousand-dollar check along with most of my cash. I signed some paperwork and after trading *sayonaras*, Andrew and I were sent on our way. I would have access to my account through the Internet, telephone, and mail, almost the same way I would had I opened a regular bank account. I felt good about the moves I had made while with Andrew. He taught me a lot in a short period of time. The whole experience was an eye-opener for me and just the beginning, as far as I was concerned.

Andrew flew back to Rome and I flew back to Miami but not before kissing and hugging for a good ten minutes. He promised to send for me again and said that I could make some more money when I came back. I told him okay and we parted ways. The long flight allowed me time to think. I couldn't believe how much money I had made in such a short time. I thought I was dealing with rich people in Florida, but apparently I hadn't seen anything. There was a big, big world outside of the Sunshine State and the little bit that I had tasted was only enough to whet my appetite. Even after dessert, I was hungry for more.

CHAPTER 8

The saying "You don't miss a good thing until it's gone" came to mind when I got back to Chatman's house. Seeing Ryan for the first time after a month reminded me of the feelings I had for that boy. I felt such an attraction to him the minute I walked in the door.

"Um, excuse me," I said, clearing my throat as a signal for Ryan and A.J. to come assist me with my luggage.

Ryan paused the video game he and A.J. had been playing and got up to help me. But the only muscles A.J. moved were the ones in his fingers as he brought a handful of tortilla chips to his mouth.

"Thank you, *Ryan*," I said.

"Oh, that's supposed to make me feel bad?" A.J. retorted sarcastically.

"That's impossible," I countered. "You're probably the only guy I know who would let your own mom carry her own groceries."

"Uphill and everything." A.J. laughed.

"You ignorant," Ryan butted in, carrying my two biggest pieces up the stairs.

I was following behind him with my carry-on bag. "I see somebody been lifting weights," I commented on Ryan's newly chiseled biceps.

He smirked and said, "I've been doin' a little somethin'."

That was an understatement. Ryan looked like he was training to be a body builder. I must say I was getting turned on by his new athletic physique.

"So," I began when we got in my room, "what all has happened since I been gone?"

"Ain't been too much. Just a lot of running around crazy tryin' to get ready for this new shipment coming."

"Oh, what's up with that anyway? I know the last time we talked, you said you were hoping to be in charge on this one."

Ryan sat down on my bed. "Yeah, so far so good. I set up everything, pretty much, the flights, the docs. All A.J. had to do was schedule pickups."

I smiled and congratulated Ryan.

"Yeah, so now it's just a matter of waiting."

"When is it arriving?" I probed.

"September eleventh."

"Oh. That's next month."

"Yeah."

"So, what is Chatman doing with all the girls he already has? Is he selling them?"

"Only a few," Ryan informed me. "We're only replacing, like, seven this time."

"I feel sorry for whoever is being replaced," I said, confident that I wasn't one of them.

As if he were reading my mind, Ryan quizzed, "How you know you're not one of them?"

"Because I just put seventy-five thousand in Chatman's account."

Ryan sighed. "Don't remind me."

I blushed. "Do I sense jealousy?"

Ryan didn't say anything, just looked away. I could have pressed the issue but I chose to leave it where it was. Even though we were broken up, I knew Ryan had certain feelings about my having gone away with a guy for a whole month, work or not. But I did find it cute that he let his feelings show. I wondered if he still liked me because I knew I still liked him. I had gotten over what he had done to me. I understood his position and I was partly to blame. As far as I was concerned, we could have gotten back together. It seemed as though Ryan wanted that. I was just waiting for him to ask.

"Yo, Ryan! Hurry up, damn!" A.J. yelled upstairs.

Ryan hopped up off my bed. "Oh shit," he said. "I forgot about that game."

"Thanks for your help," I hurried and told Ryan before he darted out of my room.

I started unpacking and putting all my stuff in its place. I missed Rome and all its excitement, but I was happy to be back in Miami.

As soon as I got back Chatman had clients lined up for me. There were a few well-off Tampa and Daytona Beach doctors and CPAs in the lineup, but what interested me most was the rapper who wanted me to accompany him to the upcoming *Source* Awards. I didn't know how to act. Chatman told that he had gotten a call from the rapper's assistant requesting me for the entire day. He only offered five grand and Chatman took it because he said that he didn't want to break the rapper's balls. Plus, he felt like that one client would most likely bring him a slew of other clients of his caliber and it would pay off in the long run.

Chatman sent me on a shopping spree to get ready for my first famous date. I bought a Roberto Cavalli dress and a pair of Versace shoes. Chatman's friend at Cartier hooked me up with some fabulous jewels. I also bought a simple Marciano dress suitable for an after-party just in case.

Monday, August 20, came and I was on my way out the door. Ryan was out meeting with some people, preparing for his shipment, otherwise he would have been there to help me take my bags to the car. I was kind of glad he wasn't there, though. He probably would have been green with envy seeing me go out with a big-time rap star, especially since he was one of Ryan's favorites. I wouldn't want to put him through that, even though at times I felt like he deserved it.

The plan was for me to stay at a hotel near the venue and I would get picked up by my date and his driver close to show-time. I was driven to a three-star hotel and checked into a small rinky-dink room with basic cable and horrible room service. It was despicable for such a highly paid entertainer who boasted about the good life to give me such accommodations.

When my date arrived, my snooty attitude vanished and I became starstruck. I couldn't believe I was chosen to be on the arm of one of the hottest guys in hip-hop. I tried to maintain my composure as I stepped inside the Bentley Continental. I spoke to the star and he nodded. The couple of people he had with him looked me up and down, but didn't speak. I took the rudeness on the chin and managed to keep my head held high. The driver whisked us away from the low-grade hotel and pulled up to the star-studded red carpet at the Jackie Gleason Theater. I was in awe, rubbing elbows with A-list celebrities.

The awards show opened with a high-energy performance by DMX and then the hosts, Vivica Fox and Busta Rhymes, took the stage. L.L. Cool J. looked so tasty receiving the Lifetime Achievement Award and Mary J. Blige tore it up. I had to give credit, the awards show was much more entertaining and well-organized compared to what I had witnessed on TV the year before. I had a good time despite the not-so-star treatment I received from my arrogant sponsor. But I was there to do a job and I did it.

We ended the night at the five-star hotel where my date had suites. Of course we had sex but it was nothing like I had imagined. It was rushed and sloppy, and I could have done without. I felt so used when it was all over. I was given five thousand in hundred-dollar bills and told good night. Then my one-time favorite rapper popped E pills and drank bottles of Hennessy until he passed out at about four in the morning. I was dropped off home at about eight and, though I was drained and ready to jump in the bed, I had to take a shower. There was no way I was going to lie down in my bed and transfer the drunken sweat and musk from my date to my sheets. The thought of it made my skin crawl. Who would have known that a date with my fantasy man would turn out to be so nightmarish? Life was tricky that way, I was learning, and as was the case in any situation, it could have been worse.

A few weeks later, I had come home from an overnight date and saw Ryan sitting outside talking on his cell phone, in obvious distress. I wanted to ask him what was wrong, but I figured I'd wait until he ended his call. I walked past him and gave him a look to ask if everything was all right. He shook his head and started pacing, his phone on his ear.

I stayed out there with him, trying to get an idea about what was going on. Then A.J. came barging out the front door.

"This shit is crazy," A.J. said.

"What?" I asked.

"You ain't heard about it?"

"Heard about what?"

"These planes hit the World Trade Center and the Pentagon this morning. They're saying it was a terrorist attack. They hijacked, like, four planes and used them as bombs."

"Oh my God, are you serious?" I asked.

"Yeah, it's all over the TV and the radio. Now they're landing all planes and not allowing anybody to fly. It fucked up our shipment."

"Oh my goodness," I sighed.

I looked back at Ryan, who was yelling through the phone. I felt bad for him, knowing how hard he had worked on getting things ready for this new shipment. This was his chance to show Chatman he could handle the duty and for reasons beyond his control he would probably fail.

"Fuck!" Ryan shouted while slamming his phone closed. *"I cannot believe this!"*

"What did he say?" A.J. asked Ryan.

"It ain't goin' to happen," Ryan said with hopelessness in his tone.

"I'll let Chatman know," A.J. said, going back into the house.

"Sorry about what happened," I told Ryan, trying to offer support. "But it's not your fault that we had a terror attack. I mean, who could have planned for this? I'm sure Chatman won't hold it against you. I'm sure he'll understand."

"I know," Ryan said. "It's just that this was my shot."

"You'll be granted another opportunity," I told him, rubbing his back.

"Yeah, maybe, but you know the next time we'll be planning another shipment?" Ryan didn't wait for an answer. "Not for, like, another three years."

"So? That just means you have three years to perfect it."

"That's if you're looking on the bright side of things."

I smirked. "That's the only side we should be looking on. Hell, the gloomy side is a given."

A.J. appeared in the doorway. "Chatman said when he gets back he wants us to meet him at the marina."

"When will that be?"

"About a week."

"Was he pissed?"

"I couldn't tell."

Ryan folded his arms and bowed his head. To him it was the end of the world, but then again, could it have been? I went inside the house to catch the news about the attacks. All the girls who were home were surrounding the sixty-inch plasma in the family room. I was in disbelief, watching the footage of two airplanes crashing into the Twin Towers. I fought tears, seeing people jumping from the buildings. Memories of my father being thrown from the plane surfaced and a void filled my heart. I felt for every man, woman, and child that day; I knew what it was like to go through such terror.

A week had gone by and America was a changed nation. There had been so much tension, political talk, and setbacks that Chatman felt we all could use a break. He had planned a surprise twenty-first birthday bash for Ryan on his yacht. I was responsible for getting the girls there. A.J. would bring Ryan. It started right around sunset. Chatman had it catered with nothing but seafood—any- and everything that lived in water was available from alligator to shark. There was so much alcohol I wouldn't have been surprised if Chatman needed a liquor license to have the party. It was wildly decorated with black and silver balloons and a banner that read HAPPY 21ST.

Ryan was scheduled to arrive close to six. He thought he and A.J. were meeting Chatman to discuss the failed shipment. He just knew he would be walking into his termination. He had told me earlier that day that he was nervous and that if he didn't come back to the house he wanted me to know that he would always love me. I grew tearful when he said it, partly because it was the first time he had ever told me that and also because I was laughing so hard inside. It was hilarious that he thought he was going to get fired when in fact he was going to celebrate his birthday.

It was a little after six. Everybody who was invited was on board. We were all just waiting for the birthday boy, me especially. I was dressed in a white tunic that hit the middle of my thighs. Under it, I had on a silver bikini that I complemented with a pair of silver, strappy four-inch stilettos. My hair was pulled back into a long slick ponytail with a small pomp in the front and my makeup was soft and natural. I looked pristine.

By the time Ryan showed up I had already had three drinks and was feeling tipsy. Just the look on his face when everybody yelled surprise turned me on. He was so relieved when he found out the real reason Chatman wanted to meet with him. After he made his rounds, greeting and thanking people, he found his way to me.

"You knew about this and didn't say anything?"

I grinned and nodded. "Yup."

"And you knew how much I was sweatin' about comin'. You could have given me a hint or somethin'."

"Maybe I liked seeing you sweat," I told him flirtatiously.

He smiled and gazed into my glassy eyes. We had a brief but strong connection like we were the only two people on the boat. The party noise seemed to cease while we stared at each other. I felt my body temperature rise and I had so much passion burning inside of me for Ryan it was unreal.

"Excuse me, everybody," Chatman called out from the bridge. He coughed and then cleared his throat. "Now that everybody is here I think it's time we have a toast." Chatman held up his glass of champagne and said, "To Ryan's twenty-first year on this planet and to another damn good fiscal year."

"Cheers," the crowd all said as we toasted our glasses and sipped our champagne.

Then fireworks lit up the darkening sky and the music thumped. The party had officially begun. Ryan and I danced the night away like we used to when we were underage kids sneaking out to the clubs. Only this time we both were heavily intoxicated, as was everybody else. I only hoped that someone had set the boat to autopilot.

"I Just Wanna Love U (Give It 2 Me)" by Jay-Z came on and I felt Ryan getting aroused. He cut the dance short and told me to meet him in the bathroom in two minutes. When I got there, he was ready for me and I was surprised at his boldness for attempting something so forbidden right under Chatman's nose.

"I guess the answer is twenty-one," I said.

"The answer to what?" he asked me, kissing me on my neck.

"Remember that long time ago I asked you what age does a guy grow his balls?" I chuckled, leaning my back against the door of the bathroom, allowing Ryan all the rights to my body.

"Yeah," he mumbled, more concentrated on removing my bikini bottom.

"Well, I guess the answer is twenty-one." I chuckled some more.

Ryan told me I was silly and continued his foreplay. We shared about ten glorious minutes together in the bathroom and then we crept back into the party. It had been a night well spent and the start of something special for Ryan and me.

"Meet me in Vegas," Ryan breathed heavily through my cell phone's earpiece.

"What?" I asked, not sure if I had heard him correctly. I walked out onto the balcony from my client's master bedroom.

"Meet me in Vegas," he repeated.

"What do you mean, meet you in Vegas? When?" I asked.

"Now," he said. "Go to the airport and get on the six-twenty flight. Delta."

I laughed at Ryan's obvious foolishness. "I am at a client's house in Cabo San Lucas!"

"I know where you are!"

"So how am I supposed to meet you in Vegas today?"

"Tell him you wanna go shopping or something! He's sixty-seven years old. Send 'im to Bingo and disappear for a few hours."

"You're really serious?" I asked Ryan.

"Yeah! I booked your flight!"

"Are you for real?" I was thrilled but confused. I thought maybe Ryan was playing with me.

"I'm serious," Ryan said. "Between going to Europe once a month and staying with your clients in between, you've been spending a lot of time away from me and I miss the hell out of you. I want to be with you right now. And I want to be with you forever."

I gazed out into the blue sunny sky, envisioning Ryan's tiny eyes looking into mine. "What are you saying, Ryan?"

"Sienna, will you marry me?" Ryan asked, as sincere as he could be.

I was ready to scream, but I didn't want to alert my client. I threw my hand over my mouth and gasped. "Yes."

"Well, then, get on the six-twenty flight to Vegas and let's get married tonight," he instructed.

I was filled with joy, agreeing to Ryan's spontaneous plan. We said our I love yous and hung up. I wiped the tears of happiness from my face and went back inside my client's villa.

"Os-car," I sang, approaching my client from behind.

Unable to take his eyes off the golf tournament he was watching on TV, he asked, "Yes, baby?"

I walked around the couch and sat beside him.

"I hate to bother you and I hate to intrude on our time together, but a good friend of mine just called and asked if I would go shopping with her. She heard from Chatman that I was here in Cabo and it's a coincidence because she's vacationing here, too."

Oscar put his hand up and rubbed my face. "Anything for you, cutie pie." He leaned forward and grabbed his can of Diet Coke off the coffee table and sipped it. Without taking his eyes off the TV he asked, "Are you good with getting around?"

"Yeah. I'll get a taxi," I said.

"Well, have fun," he said.

I called for a cab and in the meantime I freshened up, slipping on a pair of jeans, a T-shirt, and some flip-flops. I quickly threw a pair of underwear, my toothbrush, deodorant, and lotion in my pocketbook. I checked to make sure my ID was in my wallet and I headed out the door. I glossed my lips on the way to the cab.

"To the airport," I told the cab driver.

After a thirty-five-minute taxi ride and another hour and forty minutes to check in and go through security, I made it to the gate twenty minutes early for my five-fifty boarding time.

"I'm at the gate," I told Ryan.

"All right," he said. "Call me when you land."

"I can't believe you," I prolonged our conversation. "How did you pull this off? Where is Chatman?"

"Chatman bought airline tickets back in January for the Lennox Lewis and Tyson fight that was supposed to be here this month. But they wound up changing the fight to Tennessee because they wouldn't let Tyson fight in Vegas and they pushed the fight back from April to June. So Chatman just transferred his tickets to me and A.J. and told us to spend the weekend out here."

"So where's A.J.? Isn't he gonna tell?"

"Man, A.J. been trickin' and gamblin' the whole time. I was bored, missing you like crazy. I told 'im I was goin' chill in my room for the rest of the day. He said all right and I ain't heard from him since. We're supposed to meet up tomorrow afternoon at the airport to fly back home, but until then he's doin' his thing and I'm doin' mine," Ryan explained.

I took a deep breath. "Well, I can't wait to see you."

"I can't wait, either," he said.

Ryan and I went to the marriage bureau's office. We each completed a one-page application, showed our IDs, and paid a

$55 fee for our marriage license. Then we went to the DooWop Diner Wedding Chapel and got married by an Elvis impersonator. It was the best day of my life.

After the wedding, we went to a club and drank and partied until two in the morning. I called my client in a drunken stupor and asked if he would mind me staying with my friend at her resort for the night. He told me that he figured I would and that he'd see me in the morning.

I reluctantly left Ryan's side to catch my nine A.M. flight back to San Lucas. A long kiss and tap on my behind was how Ryan sent me off. I slept through the two-and-a-half-hour flight and was so ready to go home when I got back to Oscar's villa. Luckily, I had only one day left with him.

When I got back to Miami Ryan wasn't as happy to see me as I thought he should have been. Pretty much everybody was home, so I couldn't have a private moment with him like I wanted. However, after I unpacked and got settled, Chatman called me in his office and shed light on the situation.

"Sienna," Chatman began, clearing his throat. "First, I want to start off by telling you that I'm very happy with you and your progress and I would love to keep you around, but I received an offer that is almost impossible to turn down."

I wrinkled my face but kept quiet, waiting for Chatman to elaborate.

"Andrew, our European client who sends for you so much, has expressed interest in purchasing you from me."

I froze with fear.

"He has offered me quite a figure as well as a couple bonuses. Now Ryan is working out the logistics, but I have to tell you I'm seriously considering it."

I remained silent and it wasn't because I had nothing to say. I just couldn't find the words. I was speechless.

"Do you have any questions or any concerns about what I just said?" Chatman asked, clearing his throat again.

"I don't know what to say," I said. I would have loved to move to Rome with Andrew and make triple the money I was making under Chatman, but there was no way in hell I was going to leave Ryan.

"Well, if you think of anything I'm here," Chatman said. "I'll let you know my decision when Ryan brings me the details. It'll probably be sometime this evening."

"Okay," I mumbled and walked out of Chatman's office.

On the way to my room I stopped at Ryan's room. He was sitting in a chair with his hands folded behind his head.

"I heard," I said, vaguely speaking of what Chatman had told me.

Ryan didn't say anything.

"So what logistics is he waiting for you to get back to him with?" I quizzed.

Ryan looked at me and then turned away. "It's no logistics. He wants my opinion," Ryan said.

"Your opinion of whether or not he should sell me?"

"Yeah."

"Well, that's easy," I said, "Just say no."

"It's not easy, Sienna." Ryan grew frustrated. "He's simply testing me right now. He already knows his answer but he wants to see if I would make the right business decision or if I'm gonna let our personal relationship get in the way."

I was baffled. "But, he doesn't know anything about our personal relationship."

"Not as much, no, but, come on, it's no secret that we have feelings for each other. Everybody notices it."

"Okay, let's say that is the case. You can still say no."

"Not if I want to secure my position. If I say no, he'll never trust that I can handle running his business when he gives it up. Do you know how many people he has working for him who would love to take over and who have way more experience than me? I'm replaceable right now, Sienna, and the wrong move on this one thing can make all the difference."

I couldn't believe what I was hearing from Ryan. "So this decision is difficult simply because you want to prove to Chatman that you're capable of taking over his business? You mean to tell me that I'm not the important factor here?"

"Sienna, this is not the time for an argument. You know you're the important factor. But if I say no and he sells you anyway because it's the better business move then where does that leave us? We'll both be out the door. I know how he thinks."

"You don't know how he thinks! You're naïve if you believe that this is about you. Chatman is about Chatman. He's not going to get rid of you because you're cheap labor, and he's not going to get rid of me because I make him a lot of money! He's not testing you, Ryan! He has no intentions of putting you in the top spot. That's just his way of keeping you around, keeping you working hard for next to nothing. A.J.'s been his right-hand man since forever. Don't you think if Chatman puts anybody in charge of his multimillion-dollar empire it will be him?"

Ryan sat up and put his hands on his knees. "Well, since you seem to have all the answers, what do you suggest I do?"

"Tell 'im no," I said.

Ryan shrugged his shoulders and raised his palms. "Tell him no and that's it? No explanation, nothing?"

"Tell him that it wouldn't be smart to give up his highest-paid girl," I said, my mind spinning, trying to come up with a solution. "Tell him that whatever Andrew offers to buy me for he knows he can make at least double that once he has me in his possession, so it would be best to hold on to me. But Chatman should make a counteroffer that Andrew won't be able to refuse."

Ryan was intrigued, but confused. "I don't get it."

"Tell Chatman to offer Andrew the right to sell me on the side while I'm with him. This way, Andrew can make whatever money he plans on making off me without the worry of what Chatman would do if he found out, and in turn, Chatman can either take a percentage on the back end or charge more on the front end."

Ryan was deep in thought, retaining the information I was feeding him. He started nodding his head slowly. "That could work," he said.

Ryan was in Chatman's office for a little over an hour that evening after dinner. I was in my room biting my nails the whole time. When Chatman's office door finally opened, I anticipated hearing my name called. When it was, I took a deep breath and walked into Chatman's office.

"Well, Ryan and I decided that it would be best for me to keep you and just add some bells and whistles for Andrew," Chatman said, "With that said, Sienna, congratulations, you are officially my top girl."

CHAPTER 9

*A*ndrew wasted no time taking advantage of his new role as middleman in my career. Immediately after he and Chatman negotiated a deal in which they would both benefit from selling me, Andrew brokered a date with Tomio, the Japanese bank officer that he had introduced me to in Switzerland when I was opening my bank account two years ago. Apparently, Tomio had gotten in touch with Andrew and requested that I accompany him to the World Cup that was being held in Japan for the first time. Andrew collected some thousands of dollars from Tomio and put him in touch with Chatman. Chatman didn't ask any questions either as long as Tomio's forty-thousand-dollar check cleared.

When I was told that I was being sent to Japan, I was shocked. I mean at first I couldn't remember Tomio. Then when Chatman told me I had met him through Andrew, it clicked. *I guess I did lay it on him kind of strong,* I thought, reflecting on the day I impressed Tomio by greeting him in his native tongue. *I could have said "konnichiwa," the easiest Japanese greeting to remember, or, hell, I could have just said hello. It wasn't like he didn't speak English. But I opted for "good morning" instead, and the polite version at that. He didn't see that coming at all and maybe he hadn't been able to get me off his mind since. I just never would have expected him to seek me out so long after our one and only encounter.*

"Japan?" Ryan asked, sitting on my bed looking through a magazine. "What do you be doing to these men? None of the other girls get sent to places like Italy and Japan. And none of them damn sure don't get the type of checks you get. You must really be turnin' dudes out," Ryan said with jealousy in his tone.

I stopped putting my clothes in my suitcase and looked up at him. "I don't think it's that at all," I said, defending myself. "I mean, these men can get good sex from anywhere and that's the thing—with me it isn't just about sex. It's about charm and charisma. It's about intrigue. I give these men something to think about. Sometimes they don't even want sex. Sometimes they're satisfied with just having me in their presence or having me on their arm at a special event. I have a lot to offer, and you seem to be the only one who overlooks that."

Ryan put the magazine down and straightened his back from its previous slouched position. His eyebrows bent and, keen eyes glued to me, he asked, "What's that supposed to mean?"

I stood up from my kneeling position on the floor and walked over to Ryan, standing in between his legs. I poked him in the chest seductively and explained, "I know me going on dates and being requested by big, powerful men is hard for you to deal with, but look at it this way: you're the only one who counts. Plus," I continued, grabbing his head and strategically placing it between my breasts, "you're the only one who gets all of me for free."

Ryan wrapped his arms around my waist, pulling me on top of him. We reclined on my bed, looking into each other's eyes for a moment before we started kissing passionately. Ryan flipped me over on my back and started undressing me, kissing and sucking on various parts of my body. In the meantime, I was undressing him, rubbing him, and pulling him into me. My body was so uncontrollable whenever in Ryan's possession. It was nothing like the sexual experiences I'd had with other men. It seemed that Ryan had a special command over my body. Like he was a snake charmer and I was a cobra.

I was completely turned on by his slightest touch, and upon him entering me, I felt a tingling sensation run through my veins. He seemed to propel forward in all the right motions, proceeding in and out as if to a tune. I was on the ride of my life, my head back and eyes closed. I yearned for more and prayed it would never be over. And just moments later, I started shaking like I had been shocked by thousands of volts of electricity. My eyes released a few tears as Ryan continued to dance on top of me. His moment was approaching, and right before it did we gazed into each other's eyes and for a split second I could see Ryan's soul. It was heavenly.

Knock! Knock! "Your ride is here!" A.J. yelled through my closed bedroom door.

I rubbed my eyes and blinked several times so that I could see clearly. Ryan was still in my bed next to me. He was asleep. I quickly nudged him to get him up.

"Ryan . . . Ryan, get up," I told him. "My ride is downstairs. Chatman'll be in here any minute."

Ryan jumped up, buckled on his pants, and slid his feet into his shower slippers. After checking to make sure the coast was clear, he eased out of my room. I quickly freshened up in my bathroom, fixed my hair, and reapplied my makeup. As I was gathering my luggage, another knock sounded on my door, then in walked Chatman.

"You ready?" he asked, looking me over thoroughly.

I nodded, keeping my eyes on him, hoping that he wouldn't scan the room and see something that could have incriminated Ryan and me. I wasn't quite sure where the condom was and I could only hope it was hiding well.

"Let's go," he said, reaching out for me to give him my bags.

I followed Chatman out into the hallway, and saw Ryan's room door was closed. I was surprised he didn't come out and see me off like he normally did. It was usually him carrying my bags, not Chatman. I wanted to see him one last time before I traveled to a whole other continent. I wanted to smile at him to reassure him that I loved him and only him. I walked extra slowly to stall for time, thinking that maybe he was in the bathroom getting himself together to come down. But that lasted only a few seconds. Chatman rushed me to the car.

Inside the limo, I was a little sad even after the two beautiful hours I had spent with Ryan. I felt bad for him. I figured he was upset that I was leaving and couldn't handle seeing me go, especially after what we had just shared. I imagined he thought that I was just as passionate with my dates as I was with him and that must have hurt him. *If only he knew,* I thought. *I could care less about those other men.* And that was exactly my attitude in Japan.

The New Tokyo International Airport was the best yet. It had a shopping mall that housed boutiques like Salvatore Ferragamo, Cartier, Hermès, and Bulgari—you would have thought I'd been ecstatic. I window-shopped a little bit, but I didn't go in one store. I just couldn't get enthused.

Seeing Tomio again after so long reminded me of why I flirted with him in the first place. His defined features were so attractive and he had the smoothest skin I'd ever seen on a man. It was obvious he cared about his appearance, and I guessed the wealth he inherited allowed him to maintain it quite well. I greeted him and tried to make my face read something different from what my heart felt—and it seemed that my whole stay was spent doing just that.

Tomio had taken me to a hotel in Ginza, probably the wealthiest section of Tokyo. Why he didn't take me to his home, I didn't know. Maybe he didn't want me to know where he lived or maybe he had a wife and children. It didn't make much difference to me anyway. I was busy thinking about Ryan and not even a dinner at one of Tokyo's most exclusive *ryotei*—where you needed not only reservations but also introductions, your meal was 50,000 yen, and you were entertained by a geisha who danced while you ate—could take my mind off him. Claiming to be tired, I even turned down a shopping spree at Ginza Wako, one of the oldest and most prestigious department stores in Tokyo. And to top things off, after having sex with Tomio back at the hotel, I cried like a baby. I was miserable.

The next day was no better. Don't get me wrong, the World Cup final game between Germany and Brazil at the International Stadium Yokohama was the first of its kind and highly anticipated and enjoyed by fans worldwide. I had never seen a game like it, soccer or otherwise. It was more than a sports event. It was a gigantic party. Brazilian fans danced and sang throughout the stands. Mid-game, drums were played and these women wearing bikini tops, carnival-style masks, and headdresses gyrated their hips to the thumping beats. The yellow jerseys, which covered nearly every torso in the stadium, brightened the cloudy day. Latinos from all over the world were in attendance, proudly dressed in Brazilian gear from head to toe. I must say, I felt good to be among them. Having not been raised around my people, it was satisfying getting a glimpse of the culture I was born into. But, despite the high energy, good spirits, and impeccable hospitality of the Asians, I was not feeling it.

The truth of the matter was I was deeply in love with Ryan and I couldn't shake him. He had managed to occupy my mind the whole time I was in Japan. All I could think about was him growing distant from me, and I even had nightmares about him cheating on me again. Not being able to see him before I left the house had me confused. I didn't know how he was taking my being sent to Japan. I hoped that he was handling it as well as he had handled my past dates. But there was no way to tell. All in all, I missed the hell out of him and wanted the two days in Japan to go as quickly as they came. I mean, Japan was an interesting place and was definitely somewhere I would have loved to take in, but having left Ryan on such uncertain terms it was impossible for me to enjoy myself. When the time came for me to head back home, I had mixed feelings. I was happy but felt bad for Tomio. I had tried my hardest to give him a good time, but I didn't succeed.

"Sayonara," I told him, cracking a half-ass smile.

He returned the crooked grin and didn't say a word.

I walked out of the hotel room and proceeded down to the lobby to get on the waiting Limousine Bus. I stared out the window and soaked in as much of the sights as I could during the ninety-minute drive to the airport. I was sure it was the last I would see of Japan because I doubted Tomio would ever send for me again.

CHAPTER 10

It was close to two in the morning when I woke to the sound of Chatman coughing to the point of choking. I heard A.J. shouting, "You okay, boss?" and I got out of bed and went to investigate. A.J. was in Chatman's room standing outside Chatman's bathroom door. He seemed half asleep like me.

"What's wrong?" I asked.

"I don't know. We was downstairs playing pool and he started coughing," A.J. started to tell me.

"But he's always coughing," I said.

"I know, but this time it was like he couldn't stop, plus he started coughing up blood and he ran up here to spit up." A.J. turned his attention back to the slightly closed bathroom door. "Boss, you all right?"

A.J. and I both waited for a response. When we didn't get any, A.J. opened the door and went in the bathroom. I stayed back just in case Chatman was indisposed.

"Boss!" A.J. shouted.

"A.J., what's wrong?" I worried.

"Go start up my car!" A.J. instructed. "I'm takin' 'im to the hospital."

Chatman was conscious, but he was holding his chest as if he were in pain. He couldn't stop coughing and therefore couldn't talk. I did what A.J. told me and started his brand-new BMW. I went a step further and drove it out of the garage and along the curb in front of the house. By that time, the whole house was awake, including Ryan.

"Yo, what's goin' on?" Ryan asked as he watched A.J. assist Chatman down the stairs toward the front door.

I filled him in. "Chatman is sick. A.J.'s takin' him to the hospital."

"Hold up," Ryan said, a look of urgency masking his face, "I'm goin' with y'all."

Chatman shook his head. Then A.J. said, "Stay here and manage the house. Sienna, watch the girls."

Chatman was driven to Mercy Hospital on South Miami Avenue, where he was admitted. A.J. called and told us that they were going to keep him so that the doctors could run some tests. That night no one was able to sleep. We all pretty much watched TV well into the next day. We anticipated seeing Chatman walk through the front door at any given moment, but that wasn't the case. In fact, A.J. came home about three that afternoon to get some of Chatman's personal items like deodorant and underclothes. He told us that Chatman wouldn't be home for a while, that the doctors did a biopsy and they had diagnosed Chatman with throat cancer. They planned to do X-rays and a CT scan to determine whether the cancer had spread. None of us, including A.J., knew how to handle the news. All we could think was Chatman was going to die.

The days seemed to last longer than twenty-four hours for the next several weeks. Chatman was still in the hospital and I was left to supervise the girls. I had always wanted a position like that, but not under these bizarre circumstances. Nevertheless, I stepped up to the plate. I made sure they kept their rooms clean and their laundry done. I also scanned them before every date to make sure they were dressed appropriately and their personal hygiene was intact. I knew how important it was to Chatman that his girls represented him correctly.

Meanwhile, Ryan booked all the dates. He corresponded with Chatman's clients and arranged drop-offs and pickups. He also handled the money, which spoke volumes about Chatman's trust in him. A.J. was the liaison between Chatman and his business operations, going back and forth between Mercy Hospital and home often. He would check on us and see to it that we were doing what Chatman had asked us to do and then report his findings to Chatman, who wanted to know everything despite his illness.

On occasion, Ryan and I rotated our visits to Chatman. It was painful to see him in that condition. He was connected to tubes and seemed to be losing his husky build. His appearance only confirmed our fears. Ryan, A.J., and I all believed he would leave us soon.

One night after Ryan came home from visiting Chatman he asked if he could talk to me. I folded the last of my white clothes and met him in his bedroom.

"How was he?" I asked, sitting on Ryan's bed.

Ryan shook his head. "Not good."

I exhaled. "What are we going to do?"

"That's exactly what I want to talk to you about," Ryan began. "I was doing a lot of thinking and I wanna know what you think about me and you taking over this thing if something does happen to Chatman."

"You mean his business?" I asked of Ryan's reference to *this thing.*

"Yeah," he said. Stunned, I didn't respond right away. Then Ryan went on, "You figure we're basically doing that now while he's in the hospital going through his treatment and A.J. is by his side. It won't be much different, except the failure or the success of the business would be totally on us. But given that it already has a strong clientele and a proven system, it seems it can only succeed."

I thought it over and asked, "What about A.J.?"

"I thought about that. I mean, we can include him. It would be his decision, but, honestly, I don't think there is an A.J. without Chatman."

I understood what Ryan was saying. A.J. had been under Chatman for many years and seemed to have become dependent on him. He was a soldier, not a general, there was no denying that. I couldn't see him lasting in this business without his boss, despite all he had been taught.

"So you're saying if Chatman dies today or tomorrow, me and you would run his business?"

"That's what I'm saying."

"For how long?" I asked.

"Until we make enough money to retire," Ryan said.

"Hmm," I pondered.

"It would be like a family business. Us, as husband and wife, making a living for ourselves that neither of us would ever be able to do elsewhere. We could build a fortune together and then move overseas and start new lives."

Ryan had painted a picture that ultimately sold me on his idea to take over Chatman's sex trade business. I figured we had nothing else to fall back on and with our experience and knowledge, it could work. Plus, Ryan was my husband, even though no one knew it but us, and as his wife, I felt it was my duty to be by his side.

"It sounds like a plan to me," I finally said.

Ryan lifted my arms off my lap and pulled me to my feet. He wrapped his arms around me and held me tight.

"If it weren't for you, I don't know where I'd be," he said. "You're the best thing that could have ever happened to me."

My twenty-first birthday was nothing like I had previously imagined it'd be. I didn't have a huge party and I didn't get any lavish gifts. I wasn't mad, though, because I knew the lack of celebration was due to Chatman's illness. He was out of the hospital but still very sick. It had been weeks since his treatment and he was slowly recovering. He stayed in bed mostly and called on the twenty-four-hour nurse he hired for all his needs. In the meantime, Ryan was still handling the transactions part of his business and I was still handling the service part. A.J. was the runner, meeting with Chatman's outside workers— lawyers, doctors, police officers, and bankers. Normally those workers would meet Chatman at the house, but since Chatman didn't want anyone to know he was sick, he had A.J. tell everybody that he was away putting together a shipment and didn't want anyone at his home while he wasn't there.

Things continued to flow smoothly. The dates kept coming and the money kept coming in. Our lifestyle remained stable and business was as usual, with the exception of my individual productivity. Because I had the task of supervising the girls, I had to take fewer dates. It didn't bother me, though, because it meant I got to spend more time at home with Ryan, and with Chatman basically bedridden and A.J. always on the go, Ryan and I were able to enjoy each other's company in private a lot more often. Ryan and I grew so attached to each other that eventually, neither of us wanted me to take a date at all. We just didn't feel right about it anymore and we became even more determined to take over the business. But the only thing was after his radiation therapy, Chatman was getting better, not worse, and when a call came from one of his most profit-yielding clients, I was sent on my first date in months.

Andrew was in town for a conference; actually, he was in Tampa. He had called to see if I would not only spend time with him while he was in Florida but also accompany him to the conference. I shopped for suitable attire and packed my bags with a week's worth of clothes and accessories. Ryan's jealous but determined eyes saw me out the door and into the limo. I rested my head against the black leather interior and slept for most of the four hours it took for us to arrive at the Tampa Marriott Waterside Hotel.

I stepped out of the limo and a bellboy assisted me with my luggage. I text-messaged Andrew to tell him I had arrived and he texted me back with a room number. I walked through the welcoming, palm tree–filled lobby and took the elevator up to Andrew's presidential suite.

Not surprisingly, the suite was absolutely beautiful. However, Andrew wasn't thrilled with its city view.

"I wanted bay view, but I waited too late to reserve. All the big politicians got to those suites first," he complained.

"It's still quite the view," I said, cracking a charming smile.

"Come 'ere, you." He smiled back, grabbing me and tossing me on the bed. "Where have you been?"

I didn't respond. Instead, I put my lips to Andrew's and gave him a hello kiss that was sure to put an end to his questioning. Andrew and I settled in the suite and took full advantage of the hotel's VIP amenities. We pampered ourselves with the spa services and satisfied our appetites at all four of the on-site restaurants.

One evening at dinner, the night before the conference, I decided to gather some information.

"So, what's this conference about that you've traveled such distance for?" I asked, twirling my fettuccine around my fork.

Andrew chewed his asparagus and then wiped the corners of his mouth with his napkin. "It's the first nationwide conference on human trafficking," he responded. "I'm only going because there's going to be a lot of major politicians present and I'm trying to get in good with them for some business prospects I have here in the States. It helps to have friends in high places, you know."

I nodded, but didn't think twice about his answer. It didn't dawn on me what the conference was about until I was sitting in the chair surrounded by important people, including the President of the United States. I was nervous and felt out-of-place.

I whispered to Andrew, "Why me? I'm sure you could have found someone more engaging to bring to an event like this. I don't quite fit in here."

"Relax," Andrew whispered back. "You're with me so you're fine and if anyone asks, just say you're a student philanthropist."

Andrew rubbed my hand and smiled at me. I felt a little better, but it was only temporary. Minutes into the President's speech, I became more nervous and uncomfortable.

"I appreciate you inviting me to this important conference," the President said after addressing key people. "Human trafficking is one of the worst offenses against human dignity. Our nation is determined to fight that crime abroad and at home. And that's what we're here to talk about today. I am especially pleased that today Jeb has signed into law a bill making the sexual trafficking of minors a felony in the state of Florida. I appreciate his leadership."

As the President went on my discomfort intensified. While his words fell upon everyone in the massive room, it seemed like they were directed right at me. I mean, there I was in the middle of a conference geared toward bringing an end to a game in which I was a key player. The stories about women and children being victimized by modern-day slavery haunted me. I knew and understood that I was a product of that very environment, but I saw it a whole different way. The sex trade was all I knew. I was raised in it and had been a part of it for most of my life. And even after seeing girls beaten, kicked out, sold, and being made to do things they couldn't say no to, I still felt like it was an appropriate way of life. It was the norm in the trade, no different from lawyers perpetuating the lies of their clients and fast-food restaurants serving unhealthy food. It was their business practice, nothing more, nothing less.

My awkwardness continued during the networking period of the long, drawn-out conference. Andrew was approaching people nonstop, exchanging business cards and making contacts. It was natural for everyone he approached to introduce themselves to me and want to engage in small talk. Some even wanted my stand on the issue at hand. What was I to say, except I was all for the enhanced child labor laws and a crackdown on human trafficking. Little did those crime fighters know they were shaking hands with both a victim and a perpetrator. It was quite a day.

Back in the suite, Andrew thanked me for being his date and told me how proud of me he was for handling myself so well. I wanted to ask Andrew how he could participate in such a conference when he was actively involved in the very crime the conference was against. I was sure he didn't know that Chatman's escorts were undocumented slaves like those the conference-goers were trying to abolish, but either way, paying a woman for sex and selling a woman for sex were equally as demeaning and wrong. I didn't go there with him, though, as I already knew his motive. He just wanted to make important political contacts for his business purposes. It didn't matter what the conference was about. It could have been for animal rights or global warming or to ban *The Jerry Springer Show* for all he cared as long as the right people were in attendance.

I undressed and slipped into something more reserved. I started to throw all the business cards I had collected in the trash can, but something told me to just dump them in my clutch. I was exhausted from spending an entire day holding my breath. I just wanted to chill out. I convinced Andrew to order room service instead of dining out like we had done every night before. We also ordered a movie. I slowly unwound, letting the events of the day escape my mind. Before long I was waking up to a new day and my week with Andrew was up. Not wanting to let me go, Andrew promised to send for me again in a couple of weeks once he got back home in Rome.

"Until then," I told him, kissing him on the cheek.

I got inside the air-conditioned limo, a pleasant retreat from Florida's mid-July humidity. I waved good-bye to Andrew, who watched me drive off, and anticipated arriving home—back to my reality.

CHAPTER 11

I was only home long enough to almost get caught having sex with Ryan. Chatman had stayed up one night, plotting a new shipment, and barged into Ryan's room at around four in the morning to tell him his plans. Ryan had just pulled out of me, leaving my insides moist and aroused.

Just before Chatman flicked the light switch on, I buried my whole body under Ryan's comforter. Ryan placed a couple of pillows on top of me to camouflage the lumps.

"Ryan," Chatman said, "Get up a minute."

"What's wrong?" Ryan asked.

"Nothing's wrong," he said. "I just need to talk to you about a new shipment. Get up. We need to go in my office."

I felt Ryan moving around and the comforter going along with him. My heart was pounding as I thought of the punishment I would suffer once Chatman saw me in Ryan's bed. I knew Chatman was still in the room because I hadn't heard him leave. With him standing there watching Ryan get out of the bed, it was inevitable that he would catch us. Ryan would have had to move very slow and careful to keep the comforter from revealing any parts of me and that's just what he attempted.

"Why are you movin' so slow?" Chatman asked, apparently irritated. "I been up all night putting this plan together *and* I have cancer. You, on the other hand, have youth in your favor and a good night's rest in you. I should be the one dragging my feet. Let's go."

Ryan had no choice but to jump out of the bed. When he did, I felt a draft on my ankles as the comforter slid off them. Just then the light went off and I heard footsteps walking down the hall. Chatman didn't notice. I was relieved, but not relaxed. I peeked out of Ryan's door down the hallway and when Chatman's office door closed I tiptoed out of Ryan's room and into my own. It was a close call and a reality check. Now that Chatman was back home, sick or not, Ryan and I had to return to being more discreet.

The next afternoon Ryan and I both were packing our luggage. I was preparing to go to Europe as Andrew had made good on his promise and sent for me. He paid Chatman $3,600 per day for seven days, with the intention of making almost twice that per day selling me to his friends and colleagues. Ryan was on his way to Mexico where he was in charge of putting together a shipment of young poverty-stricken Mexican girls. He was very excited about having the opportunity to handle this shipment because it gave him a chance to make up for the last one he planned that failed. Chatman had decided to go back to using cargo ships to smuggle women, as the airports had become more restrictive since 9/11.

Ryan would be gone for ten days and he had an agenda for each day. He ran everything past me to get my opinion on his plan, but I think he was really just trying to show me how thorough he was. I must admit, his plan was faultless. I couldn't have constructed one better myself. He would land in Mexico and meet with a school official at the Isaac Ochoterena Middle School in Tehuacán. He would let the official know that he was a U.S. schoolteacher who was offering a study abroad program for girls between ages thirteen and sixteen. He would give the official a handful of brochures made up by none other than Sammy and tell the official to pass them out to the students. Interested students would then have their parents contact Chatman through a toll-free 800 number. Chatman would have one of his Spanish-speaking working girls tell the parents of the great opportunities that are available to their children in the study abroad program and that they would be paid generously if their child participated.

Out of about one hundred students, Chatman would hope to get yeses from at least fifty and out of the fifty Ryan would arrange for only twenty to be brought to Miami, depending on their levels of attractiveness, build, personality, and skills.

When Ryan gave me the details, I couldn't help but think about the conference I'd gone to with Andrew. The methods that people like Chatman used to lure young girls to the United States to work for them was misleading and flat-out wrong. But, on the other hand, from what I understand, those girls would damn near do anything to get to the United States, so for them the trade could be a win-win.

"Good luck," I told Ryan, who was putting his passport in the inside pocket of his blazer.

"Thanks," he said nonchalantly.

"I'm going to miss you," I told him, hoping to cheer him up.

"Me too," he said, still dry.

I rolled my eyes. "You're mad that I'm going," I figured.

"Not mad. Just uneasy," he said, not looking at me once.

"Well, you said it yourself, when Chatman hands this business over to you I won't have to go on another date." I paused to wait for Ryan's response and when it never came I said, "So let's stick to the script and make that happen."

Ryan stopped pretending to be preoccupied and looked up at me. He stood up from the chair in his room and slowly walked toward me.

"That's what I'm going to do," he said. "I promise you that."

Just as Ryan moved in to kiss me, A.J. appeared in the doorway. "Time to go," A.J. told Ryan, looking at me strangely.

"Well, there's your boarding pass you wanted me to print for you," I said, pointing to a blank piece of paper that was lying on Ryan's desk. I leaned down and folded it, then put it in Ryan's hands. "Have a safe trip," I told him, watching him and A.J. leave the room.

"You, too," Ryan said softly.

Andrew had a booked itinerary for me. I had been all over Italy and some parts of France during the week I was with him. My ability to speak French and Italian made me a favorite among his peers, and it seemed every one of them wanted a piece of me. I found myself being passed around like a bag of nachos at a Super Bowl party. From a well-known fashion designer to a young prince, I was the talk of Europe. At first I was fascinated by the attention I was getting from such notable men. Then it became tiring. They all called me Nicole Richie and kept asking me where was Paris. By the fourth day I was over the trip and counting down the days until I would be flying back to Miami. I didn't even go to Switzerland to deposit the money I had made. I was just ready to go home.

It was about seven at night when I finally unpacked and put a load of clothes in the washer. I had $27,000 to hide and figured the attic would be my best bet, at least temporarily. I could put it in my account in a month, which was when Andrew told me he would send for me again. Chatman and A.J. were out meeting with their coast guard connect and Ryan was still in Mexico.

Inside the attic, I found a bag of clothes that I had placed up there years earlier when I was planning to run away. The memories made me laugh. Taking the clothes out of the bag, I was reminded of my club-hopping days. Then as I unfolded one shirt, the tiny framed picture of my mom that Chatman had given me one year for my birthday fell onto my lap and my laughter turned into tears. I leaned my back against a small portion of wall space and squinted to see my mom's features in the dimly lit attic. I wiped my eyes numerous times before I gave up and just let the tears flow. My head against the wall, I turned in the direction of the attic door that led to Chatman's office. In the distance I saw what appeared to be photo albums and I was curious.

I crawled over to the pile of picture books and opened one. I quickly skimmed through it, realizing that it was filled with dated photographs of people I didn't know. The second book had a few pictures of Chatman and A.J. and lots of foreign women who I guessed were former workers of Chatman's. I got to the third book and never got a chance to look at the pictures because as soon as I opened it, a bunch of opened stamped envelopes fell out. They were all addressed to Chatman in an elegant cursive handwriting. The return address didn't appear to be in English, but what I did make out was that the letters had been sent from the Dominican Republic.

I dumped the envelopes and started reading the letters. They were dated as far back as 1988, the year my father was killed.

> *Dear Chatman,*
> *If you have a heart, please return my daughter to me. Or bring me back to America to be with her. I will continue to work for you and I will never disobey your rules again. I promise.*

> *Chatman,*
> *If you are reading this I am begging for your forgiveness. I should not have been with Robbie. I know how much you despised that. I am deeply sorry. Please send for me.*

Then one letter went more into detail and there was no doubt in my mind that the letters were from my mom.

> *Dear Chatman,*
> *We've wronged you, I know, but that was no reason to do what you've done. A man and a woman should be free to love whom their hearts allow. You owned me, yes, but you didn't own my love. And Robbie was a great man and a wonderful father. You know that. You were his best friend and business partner. He didn't have to die that way. I know it was you who ordered his murder and I*

have hate in my heart for you because of it. My daughter
should not have had to witness such a sight. I pray that
in your death you get your punishment and my daughter
returns to me safe and sound.

I scanned the other letters, which were basically reiterating my mom's hateful feelings toward Chatman. And none shocked me more than the last one I came across, dated in 1998, two years *after* Chatman told me my mom had been killed.

> *Chatman,*
> *You can try all you want, but you cannot keep me*
> *from my daughter. I will keep fighting for her. And I*
> *know that once she gets of age she will fight for me, too. I*
> *know you have a lot of power but the only power I believe*
> *in is my God's. I will see my daughter again!*

At the sound of Chatman and A.J. entering the house, I folded the letters and returned them to their place in the photo album. I quickly hid my money in the bottom of the bag that stored my clothes, climbed down out of the attic, and hurriedly went inside my bedroom.

"Sienna!" Chatman strained to call out. "What's all that noise?"

"I'm washing clothes!" I called down to him, disgusted at even the sound of his voice.

It was amazing how the letters I had found instantly put a nasty taste in my mouth for someone I had grown to care about for so many years. Disdain immediately took the place of love and I loathed the man who had raised me and had given me so much. All that time I thought I was in good hands—that Chatman was the man who had rescued me from my father's killer, but instead, *he* was my father's killer. Crazy thoughts flooded my mind. I wanted to kill Chatman in his sleep. I wanted to poison his food. I wanted to set him on fire. Anything that would avenge my father's murder. I was raging with emotion. My heart felt like it had swelled to three times its size and caused my chest to bulge. At that moment I could have confronted Chatman fearlessly. How dare he take my father from me and then lie about my mom being dead?

I picked up my cell phone and dialed Ryan's number. *Please pick up the phone,* I thought as the ringing began. My knees were knocking as I sat on the edge of my bed, fists balled in anger. When Ryan's voice mail sounded tears rolled down my face. I needed Ryan so badly at that point. I needed somebody to talk to.

I left a message. "It's me. Call me back."

Then I paced my bedroom, putting everything into perspective. Why would Chatman do that to my dad, especially if he was his best friend like my mom's letter claimed? That would be like him ordering A.J.'s murder or Ryan's or mine. I've known him to be stern and punish hard, but he also had a side to him that was sweet and loving. He appeared to be someone who took care of those close to him. But then again, when anyone crossed him or disobeyed him he could turn into another person. But even then I couldn't see him murdering them. Now torturing them, yes, or selling them or putting them out on their ass with nothing; but killing them, no. It was rumored that he'd had Stephen killed when it came out that he raped me, but I didn't know. I was confused. I mostly believed the words of my mother and I needed desperately to get out of the house and away from Chatman.

I made an international call to Andrew.

"Andrew," I whispered into the phone.

"Yes?" Andrew answered in an irritated and sleepy tone.

"Are you sleeping?" I asked.

"Of course I am. It's two A.M." Andrew responded.

"Oh, I forgot about the time difference. I am so sorry. I'll call you tomorrow," I said, feeling embarrassed.

"Please do," Andrew said, hanging up in my ear.

I slammed my cell phone shut and cringed. I was an emotional wreck with no outlet to dump my feelings into. I couldn't stand to be in the same house with Chatman and urges to hurt him overwhelmed me. It was bound to be one sleepless night.

CHAPTER 12

When I awoke Chatman was standing in my doorway staring daggers at me.

"Sienna," he said in a calm but eerie tone. "What were you calling Ryan for last night?" he asked, holding up Ryan's cell phone.

Had I had time to think or at least been awake for some time before being asked that, I may have been able to come up with a good excuse. But neither was the case, so I said, "I wanted to talk to him."

"For what?!" Chatman asked.

My anger at Chatman returned. I wanted not only to stop his interrogation; I wanted to hurt him.

"I was bored. Can I go back to sleep now?" I whined, laying my head back down and turning my back to Chatman.

Chatman didn't respond, but in a matter of seconds he was holding my head off my pillow by my hair. His face was filled with rage and he spoke through clenched teeth.

"Who do you think you are, brushing me off like that? Have you forgotten who's boss around here? You may have made it to the top, Sienna, but from high up it's a quick fall to the ground. That you should know. You've seen it happen to your father!"

My heart pounded in my chest and a tear escaped my eye. My mind was telling me one thing while my heart was saying another, and I lashed out at Chatman, swinging in every direction. All of my anger and frustration had been unleashed, and after several minutes I was being beaten black and blue. I took every blow with confidence, knowing that if he didn't kill me in that whipping session, I would find a way to pay him back viciously. That man had created a monster filled with enough fury to end his life, but that would have been too easy. I wanted him to suffer.

"Boss, that's enough," I heard A.J. say. "That's enough."

Chatman stopped just before landing another blow to my numbed face. Out of breath, he asked me, "Now, are we down off our high horse?"

Of course I didn't answer. For one, it felt like my mouth was missing. I couldn't feel anything in my face. Two, he wasn't looking for a response. He stood up and wiped his bloody fists on his shirt. Then he proceeded to walk out of my room. But before he made it out the door, he turned around to me and said, "You know the rules around here. You and Ryan both. I've told them to y'all more than once. Break them if y'all want. Start messing around with each other behind my back. Y'all will be in for a lot more than what y'all bargained for. A whole lot more."

Chatman walked out of my room and went downstairs. My blurred vision allowed me to see figures in the hallway, but I couldn't make out who they belonged to and how many there were. I reached up to touch my face to make sure I still had skin on it. My fingertips instantly became bloodstained. I wanted to get up off my bed and look in the mirror, but I was scared to move for fear that my face would fall off. It wasn't as painful as I'm sure it looked. In fact, I felt nothing. So I decided to just lie there until God willed me to get up, whenever that may be.

"Andrew, I need for you to send for me. If only for a few days. I will pay for it. I need you to now," I mumbled through what felt like a broken jaw.

"Sienna, I don't understand these irrational calls. What's going on?" Andrew was confused.

"Just trust me. I need you to send for me right now. Call Chatman right now and send for me. I will pay you every dime for this date. I just need you to do this for me."

"Why are you talking like that? Is this some kind of prank?"

"No. I think my jaw is broken. Just please do this for me."

Andrew grew concerned. "What happened to you? Is everything all right?"

It was hard for me to speak as it was and Andrew's questions were not making it any better. I wished he would just listen to me. "Please," I said simply, trying to keep from talking much more.

"All right," Andrew said reluctantly.

"He may tell you I'm unavailable. Just tell him you really need me and you're willing to pay whatever the cost. If he tells you I'm bruised and he doesn't want you to see me like that, just tell him you don't care, you can have me patched up or something like that. You know what to do," I told him, slurring my words.

"Okay," Andrew said, still sounding vexed.

I hung up my phone and threw some random clothes into my suitcase. I went in my bathroom and took a shower. I washed my face to the best of my ability without causing further pain. When I got out of the shower, I looked in my medicine cabinet and searched through the medications—prescription and nonprescription. I had some Aleve for pain and Nyquil for sleep. I took both. I put on some clothes and lay in my bed under the covers despite the warm summer air that flowed through my open window. I said the Lord's Prayer silently and fell asleep in no time.

It took a day and a half and a lot of negotiating for Andrew to get Chatman to send me to Europe on such short notice after the incident. He buckled when Andrew offered five thousand per day. I managed to sneak up in the attic and retrieve the money I had hid up there as well as one of the letters my mom had written to Chatman. I put twenty thousand of the money securely beneath my jeans and stockings, taping ten one-hundred-dollar bills to each thigh. The other seven grand went inside my carry-on bag. It was too hot outside for layers but I figured since that method had worked coming from Europe to the United States there was no need to change it. I was scheduled to board an early flight out of Miami, around the same time Ryan would be flying in from Mexico. That way A.J. didn't have to make two trips to the airport that day.

I felt so insecure walking through the airport, bruised to the point that I was almost unrecognizable. People were staring at me, and even airport security asked me what had happened. I told them I had recently been in a serious car accident. They became sympathetic after that, giving me special treatment, not being so invasive with me and my items while I passed through security.

On the plane I thought about how I would approach Andrew with my plan. I didn't want to give him too much information because I knew he wouldn't have been a part of it had he known all I was trying to do. But he had to know something if I was using him to execute it. After countless hours flying, I decided on an approach and an execution and even a plan B.

"Oh, dear Lord," Andrew said upon seeing me. "How did this happen?"

"Chatman," I said. "There's a lot we have to talk about."

Andrew swept me inside of his Mercedes SLR McLaren and took me straight to one of his friends—a doctor at a hospital called San Filippo Neri. The doctor, one of my previous dates, examined my face and concluded that I indeed had a broken jaw. But because the fracture was minor he treated me with antibiotics and instructed me to eat soft or liquid foods only. We left the hospital and were on our way to Andrew's house when I told Andrew my plan.

"So why did Chatman do this to you?" Andrew asked, puzzled.

"I brushed him off when he was asking me about something," I said.

Andrew shrugged his shoulders and frowned, shooting me a quick glance. "So because you brush him off, he nearly beats you to death? What kind of crazy man is he?"

"Remember the conference you took me to?"

"Yeah."

"Well, that's exactly the kind of man Chatman is."

"What do you mean?"

"He's one of the people that the conference was talking about who brings women into the United States illegally and enslaves them. He prostitutes us and makes millions of dollars off us, then sells us when we get older and buys new young illegal aliens," I explained.

Andrew gasped in shock. He took his eyes off the road longer than he should have and was forced to slam on the brakes to avoid running into the back of the Audi that was in front of us at a stoplight.

"Shit!" he blurted out. Then he quickly apologized.

"It's okay," I said.

Then he jumped right back into it. "So you mean to tell me you're an illegal alien?"

"Well, I was born in the United States, but my mother was Dominican—well, she *is* Dominican. He told me she was killed eight years ago, but I just found out she is alive. It's a lot. That's why I needed you to get me out of there. I need you to do something else for me, too," I slid in.

"What's that?" he asked.

I told Andrew everything my mind allowed me to remember. He explained that he had no idea that Chatman was conducting his business that way. He just thought Chatman was the owner of an escort service like many other Miamians and that I was simply an employee. He didn't realize how young I was—he had thought I was twenty-one when we first met when actually I was eighteen. I revealed a lot to Andrew and he to me, mainly how sorry he was about my situation. At that point, I had him in the palm of my hand and getting him to fly me to the Dominican Republic in his chartered jet took little convincing.

I had only a name and the return address on the envelope sent to Chatman years ago to work with in my search for my mother, but once we touched down at the small and unkempt El Portillo airport in Samaná, I grew anxious and hopeful.

Andrew got in contact with a tour guide he knew from previous winter vacations he had taken in the Dominican Republic and the guide agreed to help us. We traveled through some poor villages with rocky roads and locals working in sugarcane plantations. I was eyeing every person, not wanting to blink, trying to land my sights on my mom. We finally got to the address that was written on the envelope, but no house was there. The whole village seemed to be deserted. That's when the tour guide decided to tell us that my mom's town of Jimani had been severely hit by a hurricane in May, just three months earlier.

It was disastrous to walk through the ruins of the already neglected town. All my hopes diminished as I wondered if my mom really had been alive, and, if so, had the hurricane killed her. The guide was ready to get back on the bus and take us to where we started. But I was desperate to find some answers and having come so far, I refused to go back empty-handed.

I asked if we could drive through the village some more just to see if there were any survivors I could talk to. The guide told me that if we did find survivors the chances of them speaking English would be slim. I quickly put him in his place and told him that I spoke Spanish well. I was not in the mood for his unwillingness to be helpful.

Andrew pulled the guide aside and had words with him. The guide then drove us through the village. We approached every person we passed, but none knew my mom. Then as we were making our way back, about ready to end our search, I noticed an elderly woman exiting a small hutlike structure.

"*Hola,*" I greeted the wrinkled older woman with deep, sad eyes.

"*Hola,*" she said, revealing a toothless grin.

"*Estoy buscando a mi madre,*" I told her. "*¿Puedes ayudarme?*"

"*Sí, trataré,*" she said.

I got off the little bus and showed her the picture of my mom along with the letter with her name and address on it.

The lady squinted her eyes to look at the picture. Then she dropped to her knees and cried out, "Thank you, Jesus! Thank you, Jesus!"

I turned around and looked at Andrew. He was just as baffled as I was.

"*¡Ana!*" the woman shouted. "*¡Veni acá! ¡Tu hija esta aquí fuera! ¡Jesús contestó tus rezos!*"

I threw my hands over my face and cried tears of joy when I saw my mother rush out of the same hut the older woman had come out of.

My mother dropped to her knees and practically crawled over to me. "Sienna!" she shouted. "Oh, my God! My child!"

My mother hugged me forcefully, almost knocking me to the ground. The feeling of being in her arms was remarkable. I cried a river that afternoon.

Andrew arranged for my mother and her mother to ride with us to Punta Cana, a resort area of Dominican Republic. The entire ride over my mother held me in her arms. I was almost as big as she was. Her petite frame seemed to be swimming in her oversize clothes. Her mother, my grandmother, was stockier than my mother but just as short, standing barely five feet tall. I couldn't keep my eyes off my mother, remembering the day she was taken from me sixteen years earlier.

When we got to the all-inclusive resort, my mom and grandmother were so grateful. They thanked Andrew nonstop. In the suite, my mom and I started with our many questions. She asked me how I've been, how Chatman treated me, and how I found her, and I told her everything, not excluding the fact that Chatman had me believing she had been killed. I told her how I had found her letters and how Chatman had beaten me up just days before. She told me that if given the chance she could kill Chatman with her bare hands. Then she told me their history.

"Chatman's uncle ran the trade for years and Chatman was his helper. Then when his uncle passed on, he asked your dad, who was his best friend, to help him with the business. Your dad did it, but only because Chatman needed help. He didn't agree with Chatman's business practices and he would tell Chatman this all the time, but Chatman dismissed him. When Chatman got his first shipment after his uncle passed, he put your dad in charge of it. Your dad didn't want to treat the girls like Chatman did and so he was extra nice to them. He wound up getting real close with one and she had a baby by him.

"Chatman was furious and he demanded that neither your dad nor any workers were to go near any of the girls, let alone have a relationship with them. He said it was taking away from his business and from his money—that girls who weren't virgins were worthless and if they had babies they were worth even less. So when me and your dad got together we had a low-key relationship and then I wound up pregnant." My mother chuckled. "Ladies were your dad's weakness. He had no business working in the trade. Chatman knew it but was too greedy and selfish to hire somebody he actually had to pay."

"So you're saying that I have a brother or sister out there somewhere?" I asked, backtracking through my mother's story.

My mom nodded. "You have a brother," she said. "He was sent back to his mother's country when he was born. That really devastated your dad. He said that he refused to go through that again, so when we realized that I was pregnant with you, he arranged for us to run away together. He set up an apartment for us and we stayed there for close to five years before we got word that Chatman found out." My mother started to tear up. "That's when your dad decided to take us across the country. He signed up for the army, we got married, and a house was waiting for us in Houston, Texas. And that's when it all fell apart. He trusted the wrong people to fly us out of Florida."

By that time I knew just about everything about my father's death and how it occurred. What I was stuck on was the fact that I had a brother that I hadn't known about.

"So do you know where my brother is?" I asked my mom.

My mom looked over at her mom, who was sitting in a lounge chair staring out at the beach. Then she looked back at me.

"As far as I know, he's in . . . um . . ." My mom sucked her teeth and placed her hand on her head as if she was trying to recall. "I think Thailand. Yeah, his mother was from Thailand. Sophia. Her name was Sophia," my mother added.

"Well, do you know how old he is?" I asked.

"Ryan would have to be about two years older than you, I think," she said. "You're twenty-one, right?"

"Did you say Ryan?" I asked.

"Yeah. That's your brother's name," she said.

"And you said his mother's name is Sophia?" I asked, envisioning a collage of moments that painted a picture in my head. I got flashbacks of when Sophia was sold and she and Chatman had a screaming match. *What about my boy, Chatman? Huh? Is that deal off, too? Please send for my boy like you promised!* Sophia's voice played in my head. Chatman's voice followed: *You act like you've been a fuckin' angel through this! You got knocked up the day you got here! The only reason why I didn't beat that baby out of you was because you kept the pregnancy from me!"*

"I was fifteen years old! I hardly spoke English then! If you wanna blame somebody, blame your fucking partner! He sought me out!"

Then Chatman stated, *"That's why he's not here anymore."*

My mind then fast-forwarded to the first day I met Ryan and he showed me the cut-off picture of his mom. *"My mom is here in America,"* he said. *"She used to live here. Do you know her?"* I remember looking at the picture and saying, *"That's Sophia."* Then the visions disappeared from my head and reality hit like a shock wave.

My mother was telling me that Ryan, my husband, was my father's son. He was my brother. I was his sister. The revelation was too much. I choked up my banana juice and had to excuse myself. My mom asked if I was all right and tried to assist me. I told her I was fine and didn't need any help. I locked myself in the bathroom of the suite and sat down on the toilet seat. I shut my eyes as tight as I could, hoping to mentally erase time.

I left my mom in the Dominican Republic, but with Andrew's help, she and my grandmother were able to stay in the suite in Punta Cana. She didn't want me to go, especially not back to Chatman's, and it was hard leaving her. But I needed to get back to Miami to set some things straight, namely with Ryan. I promised my mom that I would send for her in a short while and I boarded the chartered jet.

Andrew kept apologizing to me. He was so sympathetic to all I had gone through and was willing to do whatever he could to help me. I told him that he had done enough and that I was extremely thankful for his generosity. Back in Rome, I handed him the money that I had brought over taped to my thighs and gave him permission to withdraw the $10,000 I had in the bank account in Switzerland. He refused the compensation and told me that he would pay Chatman the $20,000 for my four-day stay with him, even though the deal was for me to pay it. I was so grateful. Andrew put me on a flight back to Miami and wished me luck. That was the last time I saw or spoke to him.

CHAPTER 13

When I returned home much had changed. Besides the thick tension in the air, Chatman was now communicating through written notes. A.J. informed me that while I was away, Chatman had had to go back to the hospital. The doctors told him that his cancer had returned and that they would need to do surgery to remove his voice box. He refused the operation because he didn't want to start breathing and talking out of a hole in his neck, A.J. told me. So without treatment his voice weakened and it became harder for him to speak, and he began writing down everything he had to say. A part of me felt bad for Chatman, but not for long. The way I saw it, Chatman was getting his due.

Ryan was back from Mexico and I badly wanted to tell him what I had learned, but it seemed that Chatman purposely kept him running errands and out of the house. When Ryan was home, Chatman made sure he was within arm's reach. So for days, all we could do was exchange glances in passing. I wondered what it was that he was trying to tell me with his eyes. One morning while Chatman was sleeping, Ryan snuck into my room.

"Sienna, what the fuck did you do?" he asked me, waking me out of my sleep.

"What are you talking about?" I asked, dazed.

"He's selling you," Ryan said, sliding me a note. Then he kissed my lips and I pulled back. He stood up from his kneeling position and disappeared from my room.

I sat up in my bed and turned on my lamp. I rubbed my eyes to help them adjust to the light and read the note. It said that Chatman had given Ryan and A.J. a list of the girls he was selling in order to make room for the new girls that were coming in from Mexico and my name was on the list. Panicked, I gulped and my hands started to sweat. Then, instantly, I racked my brain trying to map out my plan B. First, I wrote a note in response to Ryan's note. I explained to him that I had found out that Chatman was the one who had my father killed and that my mom was really alive. I wanted to go further and tell him about us being brother and sister, but that was something I felt I should do in person.

I folded the note, tucked it in the waist of my pajama pants, and tiptoed down the hall. Chatman stopped me in my tracks. He didn't say anything. He just looked at me. I asked him what he was doing up, not expecting an answer, and proceeded down the stairs. I went into the kitchen and got a glass of milk. I was nervous and frightened. I didn't know if he had read me or if he really believed that I was up getting something to drink as opposed to trying to sneak into Ryan's room. I figured he was still suspicious of us and that was why he had been watching us like hawks since I'd been back.

I drank the milk slowly and then went back upstairs. Chatman wasn't in the hall anymore and his bedroom door was closed. I went in my room and went to turn off my lamp when I noticed another note. I opened it and read, *Sienna, I didn't raise you to be a snake. You have one week left here. Your time is up.* Chatman's signature followed.

I closed the note and massaged my temples. I knew two things: I wanted Chatman to pay for what he'd done to me and my parents and I wanted a way out of the trade. Then it hit me and I knew exactly what I needed to do. I went to my closet and pulled out the clutch I had taken to the conference with Andrew. Inside it were a bunch of business cards from the powerful people who were fighting the very industry that Chatman masterminded. I put the cards in my bra in case Chatman decided to drag me out of bed in the middle of the night and send me away somewhere. It had become volatile in the house, and things changed from one minute to the next. The way Chatman was obviously feeling toward me you never knew what impulsive decisions he would make concerning me. The way he'd grimaced at me in the hall, you would have thought he was going to attack me right then and there.

The next morning provided the perfect opportunity for me to begin executing my plan. Chatman, A.J., and Ryan left bright and early to make some last-minute preparations for the shipment. Sammy was the only male left in the house with me and the other girls. I guess Chatman told him to keep an eye on us, particularly me, because he wouldn't let me breathe. Even when I was in my room, he found something to talk to me about so that he could post up in my doorway. I decided to engage in some indirect snooping, and instead of participating in frivolous conversation, I got some useful information out of him.

"So, everybody is getting ready for the new shipment, huh?"

"Yup," Sammy said. "A lot has to be done."

"Well, not to be rude or anything, but if they're not flying girls in this time what do they need you for?" I quizzed.

Sammy stood up straight from leaning against the door-frame and said, "I did the brochures. Plus, I'll still have to make some kind of documentation for these girls. You know, just in case they get called on dates with men from other countries like you did."

"Oh. I guess you're right," I said. Then I stroked his ego some. "You're definitely a lifesaver around here, at least that's what Chatman thinks."

"Yeah, he's pretty satisfied with what I do," Sammy said.

"I guess that's why he let you in on this shipment, you know, like telling you all the details."

Sammy nodded his head in agreement. "Yeah, I was pretty shocked by that."

"I was shocked my first time, too," I said. "So, they're going back to the ships? Where are they docking this time?" I asked as if I was just curious.

"The port," Sammy said, going for the bait.

"Are they doing a late one or early one this time?" I continued fishing.

"Early. Six in the morning," he said, chomping down.

I got a catch, I thought, as I decided it was time to end my chat with Sammy and move on to step two.

"Ooh," I said, grabbing my stomach, making faces like I was in pain. I clapped my hand over my mouth and ran into my bathroom. I pretended I had to spit up. I started making gagging noises, in between which I told Sammy that I had drunk milk late last night and it must have upset my stomach. He was standing outside my bathroom door asking if I was all right and I told him I was fine but that I needed to take a shower. I ran the water and everything, hoping he would get lost.

After a short while, I heard him yell that he was going to go downstairs and watch TV and that if I needed him just give him a holler. I said okay and finally he left me alone. I pulled out my cell phone and dialed just about every number from all but two of the twelve business cards. I left messages for a few people and got through to a few, resulting in scheduled face-to-face meetings with the leader of the antitrafficking task force that had just been formed in Miami, a detective for the Miami police department, and one of the members of the National Foundation for Women Legislators.

I knew that Chatman would be gone for most of the day because when Sammy was babbling away he had mentioned that he would be watching the house until about nine. I also knew that Sammy was easy to get over on. I went in Ryan's room and turned on his clock radio, maximizing the volume. I returned to my room and got into bed, then yelled down for Sammy to bring me up a glass of ginger ale so that I could take my Aleve.

"Here you go," he said, handing me a tall glass filled to the top with soda and ice.

"Thank you." I sighed. "I don't feel well at all. I think I'm just going to lie here and go to sleep."

"Well, I hope you feel better," he said. "I'll be downstairs."

As Sammy turned to walk out of my room, I called him. He turned back. "Huh?" he asked.

"Can you please go in Ryan's room and turn off his radio? It's giving me a headache."

"Oh. Sure," he said, leaving my room.

I jumped out of bed, fully dressed with my shoes on.

I leaped down the spiral stairs quietly but rapidly and left through the kitchen door. I opened the garage and helped myself to A.J.'s BMW. The trouble I would have been in had anybody found out that I not only left the house without permission, but had taken A.J.'s new six-series knowing damn well I wasn't licensed, was inconceivable. But, it was all or nothing, I told myself as I boldly fled the mansion.

I drove to South Pointe Park, where I was to hold all three of my meetings simultaneously. Arriving several minutes early, I watched the cruise ships leaving Miami and got a chance to soak in the beauty of the day. I thought over everything I was going to tell the authorities and how I was going to lead them to Chatman and his workers on the day they would be going to pick up their upcoming shipment. I went back and forth with myself about whether I was doing the right thing and what consequences I would face should my efforts fail and I got caught. But in the end, I realized it wasn't just about me. It was about everybody who suffered at the hands of Chatman and all the young girls whom he was getting ready to trick into working for him. I had to do something to stop it and now was the time. At that clarifying moment, my mind wandered back in time to my tenth birthday when Samantha grabbed my arm and said, *"You're young so you won't understand this, but, out of all us girls here, you're the one, little lady: You're the one who's gonna make the difference."*

I took a deep breath and exhaled. Walking toward me were two men and a woman. I recognized all of them from the conference. They strutted eagerly with expressions of hope on their tanned faces, approaching me as if I was their hero.

We sat down on a bench, the breeze from the sea brushing against our backs. I promised to tell them everything I knew, recorded and all, but not until they agreed to return the favor. In exchange for my information about Chatman, his business, and his next shipment, they had to grant my mother; my grandmother; and Ryan's mother, Sophia, citizenship. Once I had that stipulation in writing, I proceeded to tell all.

"I've been in Chatman's care since I was five years old. He had my father, Robert Short, shot in the head and then thrown from an airplane. He had my mother deported back to the Dominican Republic, where he had previously smuggled her from. And then he took me in. He started out bringing women into the country on cargo ships. Then when there were major drug busts in the early nineties, he switched to planes. He has a guy who makes false documents for him. His name is Sammy. He's at the house right now as we speak and I'm almost positive he will testify if you offer him a deal—"

"Sammy, you said?" the detective cut me off. "Do you have a last name on 'im?"

"No. But he's so good at what he does he's probably not documented. And even if he is, I'm sure he has plenty of aliases. Your best bet would be to follow him and take him into custody. I guarantee he'll fold."

The detective jotted down some of what I said on a notepad and I continued.

"After nine-eleven, though, Chatman decided to go back to using ships. This upcoming shipment from Mexico is scheduled to dock in five days."

"How did they go about getting the girls from Mexico?" the tall, redheaded woman asked.

"Ry—" I paused and corrected myself. "One of his workers, A.J., went over to Mexico posing as a U.S. teacher giving out brochures for a made-up study-abroad program. The girls whose parents agreed to let them participate will be the ones that are brought over on the ship this Friday."

"When and where will the ship dock?" the task force leader asked.

"Six A.M. at the Port of Miami," I said, recalling what Sammy had revealed to me earlier.

"We've got work to do," the man said, looking at the other man and the woman.

"Well, we know time is of the essence," the woman said, "And you have to get back, but we thank you so much for your bravery and we wish you luck, okay?"

"Yes, thank you," I said.

"We will get to work on these leads and we promise you we won't let it be known who our source was," the woman said.

I nodded and watched the threesome walk back to their cars. They had Chatman's secured and secluded Star Island address; the meeting time and place for his shipment; as well as the names and profiles of the women and men he had working for him, including doctors, law enforcement agents, and even the coast guard member he was connected to. They were beyond satisfied to get so much information on so many prominent people, and were sure they would be able to build a so^{ld} case against Chatman and his team and set his captives f^{re}. The only name and profile they didn't have was Ryan's. H^{was} the only piece I left out of the puzzle. Now, my job was ^{lead} him away from the bust.

Sneaking back into Chatman's was easy becaus^{mmy was} sound asleep on the couch, snoring and grun^{ike an ani-} mal. I crept past him and up the stairs into m^{room. Filled}

with anxiety, I paced every square foot in my suite. My mind was on overload, thinking of what I would do next. My main focus was on getting some alone time with Ryan. I needed to tell him what was happening and I needed to do it fast.

Chatman, A.J., and Ryan came home that night with loads of grocery bags. They stocked the refrigerator, the cabinets, and the pantry. Then they cracked open bottles of Heineken and played several games of pool. Sammy joined them until he left to go home at midnight. I watched out my bedroom window as an unmarked police vehicle followed Sammy off the island. I was sure that would be the last time anyone saw Sammy. I went into the hall as though to put a load of clothes in the washer, but really to listen in on the guys' conversation. I could hear A.J. congratulating Ryan on becoming Chatman's new business partner and I almost fainted. I knew that Ryan wanted that title more than anything and he had worked hard to get it, but the timing was all wrong. I slipped in Ryan's room and placed a note in his sock drawer.

The next afternoon, the countdown began. Four more days until showdown and I still hadn't had the opportunity to warn Ryan. That day, I hoped I would. The phone rang in Chatman's office at about two o'clock right after Ryan left to run his daily errands. If it was who I thought it was, then it meant Ryan had gotten my note and followed my instructions.

A few minutes passed and Chatman walked in my room. He handed me a piece of paper. It read, Sienna, get dressed. You have a date at three.

I smiled as I put on my clothes, anticipating my "date." Per the usual procedure, I got in the limo and was driven to a hotel on South Beach. A young light-skinned guy greeted me upon my arrival at the Delano. The limo driver pulled off and

I walked inside the lobby of the world-famous hotel. Shortly thereafter, Ryan appeared from behind one of the large white columns that were part of the luxury decor. He led me to the Blue Door Restaurant. We sat at a table on the terrace and for the first few seconds we just stared into each other's eyes.

"Ryan," I cut to the chase, "you can't be Chatman's partner and you can't go through with the shipment."

Ryan shook his head and looked away. "Why not? Because he's selling you?" he asked, somewhat irritated.

"No." I exhaled. "I'm going to expose Chatman to the authorities."

"What?!" Ryan asked. "What is going on up there?" He poked my head with his finger. "I thought we had a plan, Sienna. Remember, stick to the script?"

"Yeah we *had* a plan, but things shifted. You told me yourself that he was selling me. What part of that plan was that?"

"It wasn't part of the plan, which is why I don't understand why you put yourself in that position. What did you do?!"

"I called you one night while you were in Mexico and Chatman had your phone," I told him.

"Why did you call me?" Ryan asked.

"Because I really needed to talk to you," I said. "And I didn't know that he had your phone."

Ryan threw up his hands. "So he's selling you because you called my phone?"

"Not necessarily. When he asked me about it I brushed him off and then he said some rude remarks about my father and I spazzed out. I started swinging on him."

"What?! Are you crazy?!"

"I was going through a lot. I had just found out some stuff about Chatman. He's not who he portrays himself to be," I told Ryan.

"Then who is he?" Ryan was agitated.

Tears gathered as I replied, "He's the man who—"

Ring! Ring!

"Hold that thought," Ryan said, answering his phone.

After a few yeses and nos, Ryan hung up and said, "Sienna, our time is limited." He looked down at his watch. "Now, what are you talking about?"

I tried to tell Ryan everything but somehow the words escaped me. I didn't know if it was Ryan's attitude that threw me off or what, but I didn't want to tell him what I knew for fear that he might not believe me and dismiss it as me just trying to get him on my side over Chatman's.

But I figured I would start slow and take the chance. That was likely to be my only opportunity to get the truth across to Ryan.

"Chatman is the man who had our father killed," I blurted out, tears rolling down my face.

Ryan rolled his eyes and disregarded my tears. "Oh, now you're taking it overboard. Chatman was right. You're truly a drama queen." He chuckled. Then he grew serious. "Your father died however he died, but mine died in a plane crash and from what my mom told me, Chatman wasn't the pilot." He paused, then continued, "Listen, I don't know what issues you developed with Chatman while I was gone, but can you wait to resolve them some other time? This is my chance, Sienna, and I don't understand why you're trying to ruin it for me."

"What?!" I asked. "I'm not trying to ruin anything for you, Ryan! I am happy for you! I'm glad you're making progress. It's what I pray for every day!"

"Then why are we here? Why are we having this conversation?"

"Because I need for you to know the truth! Because I need for you not to go to the docks!"

"So you're serious about rattin' Chatman out?" Ryan's squinted eyes burned a hole through me. "What kind of loyalty is that to show a man who took you in as a child and raised you up, giving you everything you could ever want?"

"Ryan!" I cut him off. "Listen to me!"

"I'm done listening, Sienna. This conversation is over," he said, getting up from the table. "Now, if you wanna pull a bogus stunt like snitching on Chatman, then go 'head. Just know that I'm goin' down with the ship, 'cause from what I can see, Chatman and A.J. are the only ones who really got my best interest at heart." Ryan's pain-filled eyes shot me a look that broke my heart. Then he stormed out of the restaurant.

How could he not believe me? Was he that caught up in pleasing Chatman that he wasn't even willing to consider my side of the story? I broke into a crying spell, only pulling myself together after a waitress asked if I was all right for a third time. I ordered a shot of Belvedere vodka, tossed it back, and left the hotel.

When I got home, I handed Chatman $800, which was the amount I had instructed Ryan to offer when he called Chatman disguising himself as a date. Chatman took it and went on about his business, not suspecting a thing. I went in my room and retired for the evening. The only good that came out of my long-awaited face-to-face with Ryan was the fact that I didn't tell him that I had already sunk his ship. Had I done that, I was sure Ryan would have alerted Chatman and there was no telling what would have happened to me then.

yan grew distant and ignored me. I tried making eye contact with him but he wouldn't reciprocate. He was programmed, it seemed, moving about robotically, doing everything he was told. His duties were winding down as the shipment day was nearing. I overheard his phone conversation with the person I assumed he'd met with in Mexico, telling him or her the flight times. It sounded like Ryan had arranged for the girls to board a private plane from their town that would take them to the closest international airport, from which they would fly to America. The truth of the matter was, the private plane was just a front and once out of sight of their parents and counselors, the girls would be transported on a ship and smuggled into the States. Whatever the case, it sounded like Ryan had everything in place.

I was getting ready for the day to arrive myself. I had numerous brief phone calls with various officials, giving them new information as I obtained it and confirming that everything was still a go. I also had to supply them with contact information for my mother so that they could arrange for her to get her naturalization certificate. Under normal circumstances I would have been ecstatic about being able to get my mom citizenship in America, but it was hard for me to get excited about the rainbow when I was still in the midst of the storm. I had so much to do in so little time, with hardly any privacy to do it.

One night I was in the attic getting my money and some other things when Chatman decided he couldn't sleep. He went in his office and I had no choice but to stay in the position I was in, which happened to be right above his head. I was scared stiff that he would hear the slightest noise. I stayed in the attic for over ten hours, long enough to hear Chatman recite his safe's combination to A.J. God worked in mysterious ways.

"Dear Lord, thank you for this food. Bless the hands that prepared it. Bless it to our use and us to your service. And make us ever mindful of the needs of others. Amen," one of the girls said aloud as we all bowed our heads.

The whole house was sitting at the dining table preparing to eat breakfast together. It was the first time we had ever sat down and broken bread all at once. The long table was crowded with food, dishes, and eating utensils. We all quietly feasted, only glancing at one another. It was an awkward gathering and a bit of a slap in the face for us girls, who were told to go to our rooms and pack up all our belongings afterward. The next day we were being sold to someone in Phoenix, Arizona. Some of the girls cried right there at the table, while others ceased eating as if they had suddenly lost their appetite. I kept eating and didn't shed a tear. I knew it was coming. I felt betrayed nonetheless, but I refused to let it show. Besides, I had a surprise of my own. And while Chatman thought he was knocking me back to start, I was ending the game. That next day I would be declared the winner, Chatman just didn't know it yet.

I was placing my items in my suitcases when Chatman came in my room and handed me a note. He walked out and down the hall to another room and another. Apparently he was giving us all a note and I was certain they all said the same thing: *Good-bye,* signed Chatman. I crumpled the wasted paper and threw it in the trash. Then an idea came to me and as fast as I had thrown it away, I retrieved the note. I opened it and pressed out the creases with my fingertips. I sat at my desk and pulled a blank piece of paper from my printer's tray. I practiced imitating Chatman's handwriting over and over until I felt I had perfected it. Then on a separate blank sheet, I wrote:

> *Ryan,*
>
> *I'm going to need you to meet Garson, a new doctor I'll be using to examine our shipment. I know you've never done this before, but considering the fact that you're my partner now, you should experience every duty there is. I have arranged for Garson to meet you at the Normandy Fountain Café at four A.M. This way you can be back in time to meet us at the docks at six. Do not approach anyone at the café. Garson will approach you. Just stay in the car and sit tight until he does. I trust you can handle this. Don't let me down.*

I forged Chatman's unique signature and looked it over word by word. It was believable as far as I was concerned. Now my only challenge was getting the note to Ryan without him or anyone seeing me.

At first I questioned myself for risking my plan to save someone who'd turned his back on me. It would have been easier and justified if I had been spiteful and let Ryan do what he said and go down with the ship, but my feelings for him wouldn't allow that. Plus, there was more to it than him being someone I loved beyond words. He was my brother, my flesh and blood, and at the end of the day, that mattered most. I knew he didn't mean any harm by what he had said at the Delano. I knew he was just caught between what was real and what was fantasy. He didn't have a chance to get the whole truth like I had, so I couldn't blame him for believing otherwise. In the end, I had to let bygones be bygones and try one last time to save him from disaster. I walked down the hall carrying a CD case. I went in Ryan's room, pretending to be getting some of my CDs, and placed the note on Ryan's pillow. I slipped out of his room undetected, at least I hoped. Whatever was going to happen next relied solely on fate.

That night I couldn't sleep. I tossed and turned, prayed and panicked. I bit my nails, I paced the floor. I must have gone to the bathroom a hundred times. All I could think was what if things went wrong? Suppose I had the docking time or place mixed up and Chatman didn't get caught and I ended up being sold? Worse, suppose Chatman got wind of my scheme and ordered me killed? Or what if Ryan found the note suspicious and brought it to Chatman's attention? The unanswered questions drove me crazy and I decided to write my mother a letter.

> *Dear Mommy,*
> *From the day you were forcefully stripped from me, I*

longed to see your pretty face again. I hoped and prayed that you were alive and well and that one day I would be reunited with you. I made a plan to run away and find you in your country and I didn't care about the circumstances, or whether you were rich or poor, enslaved or free. I was going to stay with you.

Seeing you that day amid the rubble and debris of the hurricane you survived was like entering the paradise of heaven. I cannot explain or express the feeling I had inside. I am still thanking God for such a miracle. Now that I know where you are and that you are safe, I want you to know the same about me.

If you get this letter it means that I have been sold to someone in Phoenix, Arizona, or that I have been killed by Chatman. I attempted to get Chatman put in jail and have you be granted citizenship in the United States. Get in touch with Sarah Barnes of the National Foundation for Women's Legislators and Anthony Pristillo of the city of Miami police department and show them this letter. They will help you from there.

And if you don't find me in Arizona or elsewhere, know that you'll find me in peace. I love you with all my heart and never ever stopped thinking about you and cherishing your sweet memory. I know you feel the same and I know I'll be forever in your heart.

Love always,
your daughter, Sienna

I folded the letter and as bad as I wanted to cry, tears were nowhere to be found. I think I was all cried out. The only thing I could do at that point was wait, so I did.

CHAPTER *15*

My instincts woke me from a brief sleep. My clock read three thirty A.M. I got out of bed and stretched, noticing that the automatic light in back of the house was on. I hurriedly walked over to my window and peered out. Ryan was swiftly making his way to his car, a 2004 Hummer H2, a recent gift from Chatman. He started it up and the engine roared. My heart sank, praying that the noise wouldn't wake Chatman or A.J. *At least he got the note,* I thought as I watched him sit in the car for a few minutes with the engine running.

"Drive off, goddamnit," I mumbled.

Like magic, Ryan pulled out of the driveway and disappeared into the early morning darkness.

I turned around and sat on the window seat. My heart was still pounding, but I was relieved that the first part of my plan had worked. I climbed back in bed intending to get a few more hours of rest, but instead ended up turning on my radio with the volume real soft, singing along to Usher and Alicia Keys' "My Boo." My face turned toward the ceiling, I closed my eyes and bopped my head, going into a zone. Song after song, I sang and grooved, allowing the music to take me to another place.

I was half asleep and half awake, murmuring the words to "All Falls Down" by Kanye West, when A.J.'s voice disturbed me.

"Ryan!" he yelled from downstairs.

Then I heard a series of footsteps jogging up the steps.

"Ryan!"

I got out of bed and went to the door, putting my ear to the space between the floor and the bottom of the door. I heard A.J. tell Chatman that Ryan wasn't in his room. Then I heard footsteps coming in my direction. I quickly ran back to my bed and got under the covers.

"Sienna," A.J. said, letting himself into my room without waiting for my answer. "Sienna!"

I peeled the covers back from over my head and squinted at A.J.

"Yes?" I asked, pretending he had awakened me.

"Have you seen Ryan?" he asked.

I shook my head. He let out a breath of frustration and then walked closer toward me. I got a little fearful when he reached out over my head, unsure of what he was going to do to me.

"Turn off the radio! You don't pay no electric bills around here," he said, hitting the power button on my radio.

I relaxed and put the covers back over my head. He left my room and didn't close the door. I immediately pulled the covers off and sat up in my bed. I listened intently, trying to hear all I could.

"He's not in your office. He's not in his room. He's not up there anywhere. Sienna hasn't seen 'im. Plus his car is gone,"

A.J. said. "I tried calling his phone, but it keeps sending me straight to his voice mail."

Of course I couldn't hear what Chatman's responses were, if he was even giving any. But I could imagine what he was thinking.

"Ryan! Where the fuck you at? Pick up ya goddamn phone, man. We're at the house waiting for you to go to the docks! I know you didn't come this far to bitch up on us, man! Pick up ya goddamn phone!" I heard A.J. say.

I looked over at my clock. It was 5:22 A.M. I breathed heavily with anxiety, waiting for Chatman and A.J. to give up on Ryan and leave. They'd planned to leave the house at five o'clock. Why were they still home? Were they going to wait until they got hold of Ryan? I hoped not. I needed them to go so that I could meet up with Ryan before he grew too restless and decided to drive back home. I couldn't afford a glitch in my plan. The slightest mistake could cause everything to come crashing down. My legs started to shake and I started biting my nails.

"He might be at the docks!" I yelled down to A.J. and Chatman, pulling bullshit from the top of my head.

"Sienna?" A.J. asked.

"Yeah," I answered.

"Chatman said come down here."

I walked down the stairs and Chatman and A.J. were both in the family room. Chatman was sitting back comfortably on the couch with his hands folded in his lap. A.J. was standing, obviously agitated.

"What did you say?" Chatman asked in a hoarse whisper.

"I said, he might be at the docks."

"What makes you think that?"

"A while ago, he told me that he was going to be the first one at the docks on this shipment. He said that he knew the excitement wouldn't let him sleep and he was probably going to get up real early and go to the docks before everybody just to make sure everything was going according to plan."

Chatman shook his head in disagreement. "He would've called somebody."

"Yeah, I think he would have, too. But I heard A.J. say that his phone kept going straight to voice mail. He might not have frequency at the docks," I rationed. "I know Ryan and he wouldn't have stood you up or done anything to jeopardize this shipment. I'm sure he's at the docks hoping you two will show up any minute. And I'm sure he's probably beating himself up about not telling you beforehand."

Chatman rubbed his hand up and down his goatee.

"He damn sure probably is at the docks," A.J. broke the silence.

Chatman nodded, seemingly deep in thought, and muttered, "Overambitious is what he is."

Then he stood up from the couch and headed toward the door. A.J. followed. Chatman opened the large wooden double doors and before he stepped out, turned to me and said, "If only you could be trusted, Sienna, you would be an asset to me."

"You, too," I mumbled, blinking to fight back tears. "You, too."

The door shut and A.J. and Chatman were gone. I ran upstairs and got right to work. First, I threw on some clothes. Then I began carrying my suitcases out to A.J.'s car, which I had pulled up in front of the house. I moved quickly and quietly as I didn't want any of the girls to wake up and see me. It wasn't that I was afraid they would rat me out because at that point I knew that Chatman was about to be arrested. There was nothing he could do to me. I just didn't want to cause any commotion. I was already behind schedule. I didn't need anything else slowing me down.

The last thing on my list to do before I left the house was to go in Chatman's office and break into his safe. I was a nervous wreck, trying the combination over and over to no avail. I had to stop and calm myself down before I could open it successfully. And when I finally did, it was as if I had come to the pot of gold at the end of the rainbow. There were big, banded stacks of one-hundred-dollar bills, gold and diamond jewelry, titles to all the vehicles Chatman owned, among other things. I loaded the money, all but three stacks, into a trash bag and left the jewelry behind. I did scramble through the titles and took out the one to A.J.'s Beamer and the one to Ryan's Hummer. I put them in my pocketbook.

I picked the trash bag of money up off the floor and tied the top of it in a knot. I left Chatman's office and walked down the stairs and out the front door. I got in A.J.'s car and slammed my foot on the gas. An adrenaline rush came over me as I sped away from the mansion. Driving down MacArthur Causeway, I saw police cars coming my way. Their sirens and bright lights interrupted the peacefulness of daybreak. It was bittersweet watching them rip past me on their way to the mansion. I turned up the music in the car and headed to Normandy Fountain Café.

When I pulled up alongside Ryan's white Hummer, his face lit up. He probably thought I was A.J. coming to deliver him from his light duty of waiting on a doctor. He got out of his car the same time I got out of A.J.'s and he was shocked to see that it was me.

"Sienna, what the hell are you doing here?" he asked.

"It's a very long story," I told him. "You wanna go inside and have some coffee?"

"I was supposed to be waiting out here for somebody."

"Garson's not coming," I informed him. "I'm the one who wrote you the note telling you to come here."

Ryan froze. He looked up to the sky and leaned his back against his car.

"Ryan, we need to talk," I began to break the news to him. "I set Chatman up. He's probably down at the docks right now as we speak being arrested for trafficking."

"So you did it," he said, surprisingly calm.

"Ryan, I found out a lot about Chatman and none of it good. He was the one who had my father killed."

Ryan cut me off. "And how did you learn this?"

"My mother," I said. "She's alive. Chatman told me she was killed to keep me from wanting to run away. He's not a stupid man. He knew deep down inside that one day I was going to go searching for her."

"How do you know all this, Sienna? And how do I know you're not making this up?" Ryan remained skeptical.

I pulled out the letters that my mom had written.

"I didn't go to these extremes for nothing. I did my research."

"What is all this?" he asked.

"They're letters that my mom wrote Chatman over the years dated up to two years after the day she was supposed to have been killed. They tell everything. I found them in the attic while you were in Mexico. That's why I called you that night when Chatman had your phone. I had Andrew send for me and I got him to take me to the return address on my mom's letters."

"You went to the Dominican Republic?"

I nodded and started wiping away tears. "I found her, Ryan. I found my mother."

"I don't understand. Why would Chatman have your father killed?"

"Because they were business partners and my father broke the cardinal rule. He slept with one of Chatman's girls *and* got her pregnant—not once, but twice," I said, leading up to the worst part of what I had to tell Ryan.

"What do you mean twice?"

"My mom was the second of Chatman's girls that my dad had a baby by, which was the final straw. The first was Sophia, your mom," I said, bowing my head.

I pulled out photos of my mom and dad that I had gotten from my mom and handed them to Ryan, who was still a bit puzzled. He looked at the pictures and then at me, stunned.

"They look just like me and you," he gasped.

I looked up at him and nodded in agreement. "I look just like my mom and you look just like our dad."

Ryan stared at me in utter astonishment. "Are you saying . . ."

I nodded again and cried. "My mother confirmed it."

"No." Ryan shook his head, flabbergasted. He threw his hands over his face and leaned his head back, slightly banging it against his passenger window.

I began taking all of what I had to give him out of bags. "Here," I said, handing him the title to his car and four of the eight stacks of hundreds I had taken from Chatman.

"Where did you get this?" he asked.

"It's our due," I told him. "You'll need this, too," I said, giving him his cell phone. "I switched phones with you last night.

I gave you mine with a dead battery. I didn't want you to be able to get in touch with anybody this morning."

Ryan shook his head in disbelief. "You planned this whole thing out."

"And last but not least, this is for your mother." I gave Ryan his mom's naturalization certificate. "In case she doesn't have one already," I told him.

He looked at the document and asked, "What is it?"

"It's her citizenship. Now go find her and make a new life for the both of you."

"What about you?" Ryan asked. "Where are you going to go?"

"I have to go to the airport to pick up my mom and my grandmom."

"Then what?" he asked.

Still crying, I smiled. "Then I'm going to Hollywood to be a movie star."

Ryan chuckled as tears began to drop from his eyes. "Come here," he said, reaching his arms out to me.

I buried myself in Ryan's arms and he cried on my shoulder. The time we spent crying together felt like an eternity.

I separated myself from his and handed him a stamped envelope addressed to *ASAP Legal Support of Las Vegas.*

"What's this?" he asked, wiping his eyes.

"It's our annulment papers," I explained. "I paid all the fees. All you have to do is sign the papers and mail them."

"So where does this leave us?" Ryan asked.

I wiped my tears and responded, "Free."

Then I turned around and walked to the driver's side of the BMW. "Good luck," I said to Ryan as I got in and put the car in drive.

"Thank you," he said, drying the tears that escaped his innocent eyes.

I could feel Ryan watching me as I drove off into the sunrise. I wanted so bad to stop the car and take him with me. But I knew I couldn't. I would have just been prolonging a departure that was bound to take place. I had to stick to the script. I turned the radio dial to an AM station and proceeded out of the café's parking lot.

"Breaking news," the newscaster's voice penetrated through the car speakers. "A major bust brings an end to a long and prosperous career in human trafficking for a Miami Beach resident on this early Friday morning. FBI agents and members of the recently formed Miami antitrafficking task force received a tip from an inside informant that led them to Chatman Bailey, a Star Island socialite, who had been smuggling girls and women from foreign countries and enslaving them here in Miami for more than two decades. More on this developing story coming after the break. . . ."

I tuned the radio back to an FM station and clutched the steering wheel tight. I burst out into a mixture of laughter and tears and thought to myself, *It's over. I won.*

ACKNOWLEDGMENTS

First and foremost, all praise be to Allah. Everything I am and do is because of him.

Second, my husband, son, mom, dad, sisters, brothers, aunts, uncles, cousins, in-laws, extended family, and dear friends: once again, I am ever so thankful for you. With each endeavor, you offer additional support, encouragement, advice, and assistance. I can't thank you enough.

Third, I'd like to thank my publishing house, Simon & Schuster, as well as my agent, Liza Dawson, for believing in me and pushing my career ahead at full speed. I'd also like to thank my former editor, Cherise Davis, and my new editor, Sulay Hernandez, for making my experience as a published author a rewarding one. Also, thanks to Martha Schwartz. Thanks to Jamie McDonald and Marcia Burch, and the entire marketing department over at Touchstone Fireside. Thanks also to Dawn Michelle of Dream Relations. And to anyone who had a hand in getting this book produced and in the hands of the public, I appreciate your efforts and hard work.

Thanks to Karen Quinones Miller, Daaimah S. Poole, Omar Tyree, Vickie M. Stringer, K'wan, Danielle Santiago, and other authors who have not only commended my work but also made me feel welcome in this business.

And as promised, I want to send a special thank-you to Oasis Parent Book Club. I had a ball with you ladies and look forward to visiting again.

To all my readers, fans, supporters, and anybody I may have missed, I truly appreciate you for your contribution to my success and I sincerely hope I can continue to deliver the way that you continue to support.

Thank you all.

Ya girl,

Turn the page for an excerpt from
Miasha's next novel

Never Enough

The long awaited sequel to the bestselling novel
Secret Society

available from Touchstone in June 2008

PREFACE

"She's flatlined!" a female called out.

"Come on, Celess! Don't you die on me!" Ms. Carol, my psychiatrist pleaded.

"What happened?" the woman asked.

"I left something at her house and when I went back to get it, I found her passed out," Ms. Carol explained, sounding horrified. "Her bottle of sedatives was empty beside her. I tried CPR on her. Then I just figured I'd better get her—"

"Possible overdose!" the woman shouted over Ms. Carol.

"Stand back!" a man ordered. "One, two, three . . . " he counted as he placed paddles on my chest. "Again!" he yelled.

All the people who ever wanted me to die didn't make it happen, including myself. Khalil put a gun to my face and pulled the trigger and I survived. I contemplated suicide I don't know how many times in the past, but never went through with it once. And I was almost positive there were some people in the world who may have prayed for my death, maybe even my own mom, but I didn't go anywhere. However, the straw that broke the camel's back was when Michael called me months after the shooting. His voice alone gave me something to live for. He sounded so sweet and concerned when he told me he hadn't been able to stop thinking about me.

"Michael, you don't know how good it is to hear your voice," I told him, a tear sliding down my cheek. "I am so sorry. I never meant to hurt you like I did. I mean, I was playing with fire and I know that and every time I thought about stopping it was like

I couldn't, like I was addicted to the life I was leading. I can't explain it. It's so difficult to be someone you're not and go your whole life trying to hide who you really are. All I know is that I was wrong and I wish it didn't take for me to get shot in the face and my best friend to get killed for me to learn that lesson."

I had to pause to slow up my crying and then I continued, "For what it's worth, I deeply apologize for deceiving you. You didn't deserve to be done like that, honestly, and believe me I am getting my payback. Not a day goes by that I don't think about killing myself. It's just painful, the whole thing. I can't really explain it. All I can do is keep apologizing and beg for your forgiveness."

"Are you finished?" Michael's saddened voice asked considerately.

I was crying too much to answer; besides, I didn't want to. I was anxious about what he had to say. I clutched the phone tighter and pressed it against my ear harder just to be sure I could hear him clearly. I wanted to feel like I was next to him, like he was right there on my couch, my head leaning on his broad shoulder.

"I don't know where to start," he began. "I mean, you hurt me. You hurt me bad. I can't even tell you how much it hurts. I put a lot into you, Celess. I was a damn good man to you. I opened you that salon. I just knew you were going to be the woman I made my wife." Then, anger building in his tone, he said, "But you completely destroyed all of that. You destroyed my life and you know what, I feel bad that Tina died and you didn't. Both of you were trifling, lying bitches and both of you should be burning in hell right now! You talk about killing yourself, go ahead. Even the score. You were going to leave me and move to L.A. with Tina so you might as well go to hell with her too! Think about it—don't you deserve the same punishment as her? You were both doing the same thing, running around in skirts and makeup telling guys like me you were women when you were really men. You disgust me, Celess! I really, really hope that you do commit suicide. That's the only way I'd know for sure that your ass would be burning in hell where you belong. So go ahead! Don't talk about it, be about it. Soon as I hang this phone up in your ear, slit your fucking wrist, go jump off a bridge, anything. I don't give a fuck. You could die right now and I wouldn't shed a single tear. I hate you for what you did to me! Kill yourself, bitch!" *Click.*

That did it. No one or nothing had done it up to that point. But Michael had pushed me to my limit. Of all people, he was the only one who had the power to bring an end to my life. Khalil couldn't do it with a thirty-eight. But Michael did it with his words.

THE INTRODUCTION

Flashbacks of my life appeared in my thoughts. Tina's pretty smile, money, cars, designer clothes, jewelry, and the men—oh, the men! I think I might have been smiling in the hospital bed when I thought about the men. Their sexy asses. I couldn't believe the turn my life had taken. I couldn't believe I was up in the hospital once again having doctors fight to save my life. What was going to come of all this, I didn't know. Was I facing life or death? I wondered. And if I were to survive this one, what would I do differently? How would I live my life? I felt myself regaining consciousness as more thoughts filled my head.

"Celess," I heard a woman's voice mumble. It grew louder. "CE-LESS!"

I opened my eyes slowly and blinked several times trying to adjust to the bright lights. Ms. Carol was standing over me.

"She's awake!" Ms. Carol shouted.

A nurse entered the room and began waving her hands in front of my face. Naturally, my eyes followed her hands and that was a for-sure sign that I was no longer in a comatose state. Days later, right before my discharge, Ms. Carol came to see me and try to talk some sense into me.

"So," she said, shaking her head back and forth. "What are you going to do, live the rest of your life in and out of the hospital, pitying yourself?"

"That's not what I want," I answered, depressed.

"Then what do you want?"

"I want my life back. The way it was before."

"Well, I don't know about that, Celess. I mean, you weren't living right before and that's why you're suffering now."

"I know. So really it's not up to me. It's karma."

"But you can change all of that," she said, reaching into her pocketbook. "I've been doing some research and I found out that men who go through with the sex change tend to have happier lives post-op than pre-op."

I looked at the pamphlets Ms. Carol had in her hands and didn't say anything.

"I just think you should do it. I know you want to be a woman more than anything, and you have so much more living to do. This is your second brush with death because of the same thing. How much longer are you going to allow this dark cloud to hang over you? And how many more times do you think God is going to spare your life?" Ms. Carol pressed.

I thought about what Ms. Carol was saying and she was right. I *did* want to be a woman. But I was letting my situation get the best of me. I was letting sadness and depression take control of me and I was actually getting used to sympathy. Maybe I was pitying myself, and that was no way to live for somebody like me, who'd loved life at one time.

Ms. Carol interrupted my thoughts."You're so young, Celess. You're only twenty-two years old. You have a full life ahead of you. Why let it waste away?"

"All right," I finally spoke. "I want to do it."

Ms. Carol's face lit up. "Are you serious?" she asked. "I mean, by no means do I want you to go through with this on my account. I want it to be something *you* really want to do."

"Ms. Carol, I'm tired of living this way. You're right, I'm only twenty-two. I could be doing so much, seeing so much, being so much. If it was meant for me to die, I would have been dead. God must have a plan for me. And who am I to disrupt that?"

Ms. Carol nodded and with tears in her eyes she said, "I just think you'll be so happy. I can see you being this beautiful woman with so much to offer this world."

"Well, whatever the outcome, I'm tired of risking my life for one organ. Cut the shit off," I said, plainly.

Ms. Carol went on to explain the procedure and the costs based on her research. She even gave me the names and numbers of a few surgeons. Most were out of town but they were specialists and had achieved optimum results. When it was all said and done, I took Ms. Carol's advice. I left the hospital with a mission to accomplish. I was going to be a woman once and for all.

Getting sexual reassignment surgery, or SRS, took a lot more than what I initially expected. I thought I could research a surgeon, schedule an appointment, and have it done. That was *so* not the case. I was ordered to be evaluated by a psychologist for six months—luckily, I had Ms. Carol—and a medical doctor had to determine me a suitable candidate according to the guidelines of the Harry Benjamin International Gender Dysphoria Association. In the meantime, I opted to go ahead and get the facial feminizing surgery I had discussed with my doctor in the past. I had the forehead surgery, which included scalp advancement, brow elevation, the removal of my superorbital bossing, and the contouring of my orbital rim. I also had a rhinoplasty, otherwise known as a nose job. I waited a month later to have a cheek augmentation. Then I got hair transplants. I had just completed my genital electrolysis and was ready for my actual sex change, or a vaginoplasty as it's called in medical terms. Along with that procedure I was getting a boob job the same day. I stored my sperm in case in the future I would want to have a baby. I didn't think I would—especially not with *my* sperm—but when the option was presented to me, I said what the hell, you never know.

I was nervous going into the surgery, even after undergoing so many others beforehand. But this was the big one, the one that would forever make me a woman. There was no turning back. I spent about nine days in the hospital after having my penis inverted to create a vagina. Then three months later I was back in for the follow-up procedure, the labioplasty, where the doctor basically perfected the form and look of my new vagina. The next day I was on my way back home to Philly from Portland, Oregon. I had my name changed legally as well as my Social Security number.

It took close to two long, gruesome years before I was done with all my surgeries and officially became Celess. I knew it would be a little while for me to get fully comfortable in my new skin, but when I did it was gonna be on and poppin'. Niggas thought I was a bad bitch before? Wait till they see me now, I thought. I looked perfect, like a black Barbie, and as for my face, you would never be able to tell I had been shot in it. It was right back to the pretty-ass face I had attracted plenty of dough-gettin' niggas with. All I needed was some time to get my head back in the game and niggas was gonna have a problem on their hands.

Ms. Carol invited me on a shopping trip to Woodbury Commons, an outlet mall of high-end stores in upstate New York. I didn't want to go, but she practically begged me. It was a good thing too, because it was there that I met Brad, a New York City–based photographer. He was eyeing me while I selectively picked through the marked-down items in Dolce & Gabbana. He approached me and handed me his business card.

"Excuse me for intruding, but I couldn't help but notice your stunning beauty," he said with what sounded like a Russian accent.

I smiled and took the card.

"I'm a fashion photographer and I'm actually in the process of shooting an editorial for *Harper's Bazaar* magazine—"

"I love *Bazaar*," I cut him off.

"Yeah? Well, I'd love it if you could come and do a test shoot for it. I think your look is just perfect for the story."

"Well, here, take my number," I said. "Call me. I'll do it."

I gave the photographer my cell phone number and got back to shopping. I didn't have any expectations and figured if he called, he called.

I heard from Brad a couple days later and took the train to New York that following week. It was right before Christmas in 2004.

"Hold that, yes. Great. That's beautiful," Brad guided me as he snapped away. "Last frame."

I exhaled after the last flash sparked. It had been one long day in New York. Scene after scene, wardrobe change after wardrobe change, shot after shot. I was exhausted to say the least, but my adrenaline was pumping.

"How did I do?" I asked Brad.

"Just as I expected," he responded. "Fantastic. You can get changed."

I smiled at Brad's report and headed toward the changing room. Inside were two guys who were apparently getting ready for their photo shoot. They looked up and greeted me as I entered. Then they continued doing what they were doing before I walked in. I waited a few seconds to see if they would offer me privacy. When they didn't I figured I was expected to change in front of them. The nervousness quickly evaporated as I remembered I had nothing to hide anymore. I was a woman with a well-constructed vagina, and in fact, I was eager to show it off.

I pulled off the big fluffy dress I was in, took down my panty hose, and slipped into my jeans panty-less and confident. I noticed the guys peeking and I smiled inside at their obvious interest. I even felt myself getting horny at the thought of having a threesome with them. Hell, they were good-looking young models and possibly the next Tyson Beckfords. Fucking them while they were still undiscovered could be an investment in my future. And was it ever. I ended up letting one of the guys fuck me in the ass and the other test out my new parts. It had been quite a while since I'd had sex and it wasn't until then that I realized just how much I missed it. I won't lie, it felt awkward at first, even painful, but as my nerves eased and my mind got into it, I was lovin' it like I used to.

I guessed Brad grew suspicious when I hadn't exited the changing room as quickly as I should have because he barged in like he already knew something was going on. But instead of him cursing us out for turning his studio into HBO's *Cathouse,* he asked if he could join the fun. It would have been rather rude for me to turn him down so I gave him some too. A few days later I got a call from him saying that I was chosen to shoot for *Bazaar* over six professional models,.

I didn't hesitate returning to New York, and I didn't hesitate fucking Brad once more either. As far as I was concerned it was that act that got me the gig. Instantly, my mind started to catch up to my body and I was turning back into Celess. My old theory about using what you got to get what you want resurfaced and I found a new business to apply it to.

After my photo appeared in such a major fashion publication, I started getting more print work. From there I landed some runway jobs. I wasn't the best walker, but I was damn good on my knees and I ended up doing two shows during New York Fashion Week in February 2005. I was raking in the dough and making a name for myself at the same time. Nothing could be better. I told Ms. Carol that it was all blessings bestowed upon me, leaving out the extra things I did to get where I was. I figured it was none of her business what I did behind closed doors.

People were buzzing about me in the fashion industry and by

the summer I had a professional portfolio and was offered a contract with an elite modeling agency in California. I immediately started making plans to relocate. I put my house on the market and started calling all the utility companies I had accounts with to schedule shut-off dates. In the process, I realized that if and when my mom decided to return my calls, she wouldn't get through if I had my house phone cut off. So I called her once more. I left a message on her machine telling her of my newfound success and my upcoming move to L.A. I let her know that she needed to call me quickly before my phone was disconnected. Surprisingly, she finally reached out to me. I didn't know if it was because I had told her that I was about to be famous or if she just wanted to see me before I left for L.A. Either way, she arranged for me to visit her the day before my flight out.

I walked up to my old house; my mom was out front gardening. Her back was turned to me as I approached the steps. I had tears in my eyes, looking at how slowly she was moving compared to how she did when I was a kid. It made me realize just how much time had gone by since I seen her last.

"You still have the best flowers on the block," I said.

"Charles?" my mom asked, without turning around.

I held out my hands, palms turned up, and replied, "What's left of 'im."

When my mom turned around, her eyes zoomed in on me, looking me over. Standing stiff, tears running down her face, she shook her head.

"Charles, look at you."

I didn't say anything—I didn't know how she was taking my transformation. Was she still upset or just surprised? I wasn't sure so I just stood there quietly waiting to find out.

"What did you do to yourself?" she asked, removing her gloves.

"Well," I said, not knowing what else to say. "I got a sex change."

My mom shook her head again and wiped her eyes.

"Why did you come here, Charles? Why did you even bother?" she asked.

I put my hands back down to my sides and let go of the tears that were waiting patiently in the corners of my eyes.

"Because I thought that somehow deep in your heart you would have unconditional love for me like I have for you," I answered her. "But," I added before she could say anything else, "I guess not. Sorry for disturbing you." I turned around and walked back down the steps. My mom watched me as I got inside my rented Dodge Charger.

"Unconditional love is one thing, eternal love is another. At some point you have to pray for eternal love, and doing what you're doing, you'll never get it," my mom reminded me of her beliefs.

"Good-bye, Mom," I said, starting up the car. I pulled away from the curb and promised myself that that was the last time I would try to make amends. I washed my hands of her and I was positive she felt the same about me.

FOURTEEN MONTHS LATER . . . SEPTEMBER 2006

"Oooh, I love it!" I squealed, looking at the 1,900-square-foot condo in downtown L.A.

"You like it, really?" Terry asked. "I know it's not as big as my brother's house, but, it's only you, you know?"

"Oh please. Like I expect you to put me in my own mansion. It'll do just fine," I said, hugging him and kissing him on his cheek.

Terry was an older, white, filthy rich investor I used to mess with. I met him through my best friend, Tina, who was messing with his twin brother, Derrek. Tina actually wound up marrying Derrek but due to her untimely death, their marriage was short-lived. However, Derrek kept in touch with me over the years, even contributing to my surgery. When I first moved out to the West Coast, I stayed with him. I would have stayed with Terry, seeing as how he was the one I used to deal with, but he had a woman living with him at the time. From what I got out of Derrek one night when he was drunk, she was a trans-prostitute Terry had picked up and pretty-womaned. I didn't care though. I never did like Terry. He wasn't attractive and being bald, old, and flabby didn't help. Plus he liked for me to fuck him in the ass rather than the other way around and I wasn't into that. I only did it because he was peeling me off.

"So, Derrek and I are going to help you furnish the place," Terry said, walking behind me as I toured my new place.

"Where's he at anyway? I thought he was meeting us here," I said.

"He was, but he called. One of his meetings ran over. But he told me to tell you that he hopes you like it. He went through a lot to get it. One of his colleagues had it under contract. He had to almost triple the value to get him to cut it loose."

"Well, you tell him that I absolutely love it! And I can't explain how grateful I am to him, doing this for me. You and him both have been lifesavers for me."

"Don't mention it. It's what we do, you know?" Terry said modestly. Looking at his watch, he asked, "What time are the movers coming with your things?"

"They said between one and four," I said.

"Well, it's a quarter to three so they should be here soon. I'm going to get outta here, though. I have to pick up Andrea from the doctors."

I acted concerned. "Is everything all right?" I asked.

Terry nodded his head, "Just Botox, that's all."

"Oh, okay," I said. "Well, I'm going to start wiping down everything so when the movers come they can just put things in place."

"You should have told Derrek to send Lucille by. She would have cleaned the place spotless."

"No, it's fine. You two have done enough. The least I can do is clean my own condo."

"Well, have fun," Terry joked. "I'll call you later."

"All right. Thanks again," I said, hugging Terry once more.

He kissed me on my lips. Once he disappeared, I did amateurish cartwheels throughout the open living room. I was ecstatic to have such a big condo downtown. It was my dream house complete with all the modern amenities one could wish for. Terry and Derrek outdid themselves, I thought to myself. They'd always been big spenders and after I was shot and Tina was killed, they felt sorry for me. And even though what happened to us wasn't their fault, I guess their extreme generosity was their way of saying sorry. *Keep the apologies coming, motherfuckers,* I thought, smiling ear to ear, looking around at my new home. *Keep the apologies coming!*

A few weeks passed before my condo was fully furnished. I chose black leather for my seating and glass tops for my tables. I did a winter white alpaca rug on the floor and a couple expensive paintings on the walls. I kept the decor simple. I didn't want to clutter the open space. When I was done playing interior designer, I grew bored with myself. I decided that now that I was out on my own and I actually had rent to pay, I needed to book more gigs. My agency was passing things off to me like small-time runway shows and functions and some low-budget advertisements, but I didn't travel all the way to the opposite side of the country to be mediocre. Shit, I would have been better off in New York.

I decided that I would take matters into my own hands. I knew that physical appearance was the first thing clients looked at when choosing models, and even though I was naturally thin, that meant nothing in Hollywood. Everybody was thin. You had to be toned as well. I got a membership at an upscale gym that was known for accommodating celebrities. The fees were a hefty sum to add to my already expensive lifestyle, but I figured it would be worth it. I started working out three days a week. Eventually I hired a trainer—or should I say, I used the barter system to obtain a trainer. His name was Corey. He had trained the best of the best. And from the looks of it, he was in the greatest shape of them all. I didn't know how to measure his abs, but he was definitely past a six-pack. His arms looked like boulders, chiseled to perfection. And his legs were long and athletic, making him appear taller than he actually was.

"When will I start seeing results?" I asked, examining my abs in the floor-to-ceiling mirror in Corey's personal gym. We had just completed a workout and I was dying to see the fruits of my labor.

Corey walked over to me and ran his finger across my stomach. "You don't see those muscles forming?" he asked.

"Stop, that tickles," I told him, chuckling.

"Well, would you rather it hurt?" he asked, pushing up on me.

"What are you suggesting?" I asked, backing up.

Corey pulled me to him by the elastic waist on my stretch pants. "One more workout," he said, seductively.

"Right here?" I asked.

"Right now," he responded.